| AUTHOR | CLASS | SF |
|---|---|---|
| ANDERSON | | F |
| **TITLE** We claim these Stars | **No.** | |
| | | 476016353 |

# WE CLAIM THESE STARS

# WE CLAIM
# THESE STARS

POUL ANDERSON

LONDON : DENNIS DOBSON

First published in Great Britain in 1976
by Dobson Books Ltd, 80 Kensington Church Street, London W8
and printed in Great Britain by Lowe & Brydone (Printers) Ltd, Thetford

ISBN 0 234 77946 2

# CAST OF CHARACTERS

### SIR DOMINIC FLANDRY

He'd risk death rather than lose the luxuries he loved.

### AYCHARAYCH

He held the knowledge of all men in his mind, and the fate of the galaxy in his hands.

### CATHERINE KITTREDGE

Just a good little girl from a doomed planet.

### SVANTOZIK

He was a well-trained hunter; the mind was both his weapon and his target.

### JUDITH HURST

She was a rebel with a cause — a liberal mind in a free body.

### CHIVES

The perfect gentleman's gentleman, even his long green tail was discreet.

# CHAPTER I

IT PLEASED Ruethen of the Long Hand to give a feast and ball at the Crystal Moon for his enemies. He knew they must come. Pride of race had slipped from Terra, while the need to appear well-bred and sophisticated had waxed correspondingly. The fact that spaceships prowled and fought, fifty light-years beyond Antares, made it all the more impossible a gaucherie to refuse an invitation from the Merseian representative. Besides, one could feel delightfully wicked and ever so delicately in danger.

Captain Sir Dominic Flandry, Imperial Naval Intelligence Corps, allowed himself a small complaint. "It's not that I refuse any being's liquor," he said, "and Ruethen has a chef for his human-type meals who'd be worth a war to get. But I thought I was on furlough."

"So you are," said Diana Vinogradoff, Right Noble Lady Guardian of the Mare Crisium. "Only I saw you first."

Flandry grinned and slid an arm about her shoulders. He felt pretty sure he was going to win his bet with Ivar del Bruno. They relaxed in the lounger and he switched off the lights.

This borrowed yacht was ridiculously frail and ornate; but a saloon which was one bubble of clear plastic, ah! Now in the sudden darkness, space leaped forth, crystal black and a wintry blaze of stars. The banded shield of Jupiter swelled even as they watched, spilling soft amber radiance into the ship. Lady Diana became a figure out of myth, altogether beautiful; her jewels glittered like 'raindrops on her long gown and heaped tresses. Flandry stroked his neat mustache. *I don't suppose I look too hideous myself,* he thought smugly, and advanced to the attack.

"No . . . please . . . not now." Lady Diana fended him off, but in a promising way. Flandry reclined again. No hurry. The banquet and dance would take hours. Afterward, when the yacht made its leisured way home toward Terra, and champagne bubbles danced in both their heads. . . . "Why did you say that about being on furlough?" she asked, smoothing her coiffure with slim fingers. Her luminous nail polish danced about in the twilight like flying candle flames.

Flandry got a cigarette from his own shimmerite jacket and inhaled it to life. The glow picked out his face, narrow, with high cheek bones and gray eyes, seal-brown hair and straight nose. He sometimes thought his last biosculp had made it too handsome, and he ought to change it again. But what the devil, he wasn't on Terra often enough for the girls to get bored with his looks. Besides, his wardrobe, which he did take pains to keep fashionable, was expensive enough to rule out many other vanities.

"The Nyanza business was a trifle wearing, y'know," he said, to remind her of yet another exploit of his on yet another exotic planet. "I came Home for a rest. And the Merseians are such damnably strenuous creatures. It makes me tired just to look at one, let alone spar with him."

"You don't have to, tonight, Sir Dominic," she smiled. "Can't you lay all this feuding aside, just for a little while, and be friends with them? I mean, we're all beings, in spite of these silly rivalries."

"I'd love to relax with them, my lady. But you see, they never do."

"Oh, come now! I've talked to them, often, and—"

"They can radiate all the virile charm they need," said Flandry. For an instant his light tone was edged with acid. "But destroying the Terrestrial Empire is a full-time job."

Then, quickly, he remembered what he was about, and picked up his usual line of banter. He wasn't required to be an Intelligence agent all the time, was he? When a thousand-credit bet with his friend was involved? Ivar del Bruno had insisted that Lady Diana Vinogradoff would never bestow her favors on anyone under the rank of earl. The challenge was hard to refuse, when the target was so intrinsically tempting, and when Flandry had good reason to be complacent about his own abilities. It had been a hard campaign, though, and yielding to her whim to attend the Merseian party was only a small fraction of the lengths to which he had gone.

But now, Flandry decided, if he played his cards right for a few hours more, the end would be achieved. And afterward, a thousand credits would buy a really good orgy for two at the Everest House.

Chives, valet cum pilot cum private gunman, slipped the yacht smoothly into berth at the Crystal Moon. There was no flutter of weight change, though deceleration had been swift and the internal force-field hard put to compensate. Flandry stood up, cocked his beret at a carefully rakish angle, swirled his scarlet cloak, and offered an arm to Lady Diana. They stepped through the airlock and along a transparent tube to the palace.

The woman caught a delighted gasp. "I've never seen it so close up," she whispered. "Who ever made it?"

The artificial satellite had Jupiter for background, and the Milky Way and the huge, cold constellations. Glass-clear walls faced infinity, curving and tumbling like water. Planar gravity fields held faceted, synthetic jewels; ruby, emerald, diamond, topaz, massing several tons each, in orbit around the central minaret. One outward thrust of bubble was left at zero gee, a conservatory where mutant ferns and orchids rippled on rhythmic breezes.

"I understand it was built for Lord Tsung-Tse about a century back," said Flandry. "His son sold it for gambling debts, and the then Merseian ambassador acquired it and had it put in orbit around Jupiter. Symbolic, eh?"

She arched questioning brows, but he thought better of explaining. His own mind ran on, *Eh, for sure. I suppose it's inevitable and so forth. Terra has been too rich for too long; we've grown old and content, no more high hazards for us. Whereas the Merseian Empire is fresh, vigorous, disciplined, dedicated, et tedious cetera. Personally, I enjoy decadence; but somebody has to hold off the Long Night for my own lifetime, and it looks as if I'm elected.*

Then they neared the portal, where a silver spider-web gate stood open. Ruethen himself greeted them at the head of an iridescent slideramp. Such was Merseian custom. But he bowed in Terran style and touched horny lips to Lady Diana's hand. "A rare pleasure, I am certain." The bass voice gave to fluent Anglic an indescribable nonhuman accent.

She considered him. The Merseian was a true mammal, but with more traces of reptile ancestry than humankind: pale green skin, hairless and finely scaled; a low spiny ridge from the head down along the backbone to the end of a long thick tail. He was broader than a man, and would have stood a sheer two meters did he not walk with a forward-stooping gait. Except for its baldness and lack of external ears, the face was quite humanoid, even good-looking in a heavy rough way. But the eyes beneath the overhanging brow ridges were two small pits of jet. Ruethen wore the austere uniform of his class, form-fitting black with silver trim. A blaster was belted at his hip.

Lady Diana's perfectly sculped mouth curved in a smile. "Do you actually know me, my lord?" she murmured.

"Frankly, no." A barbaric bluntness. Any noble of Terra would have been agile to disguise his ignorance. "But while this log does burn upon the altar stone, peace-holy be it among us. As my tribe would say in the Cold Valleys."

"Of course you are an old friend of my escort," she teased.

Ruethen cocked an eye at Flandry. And suddenly the man sensed tautness in that massive frame. Just for a moment, Ruethen's whole body became a mask. "We have met now and then," said the Merseian dryly. "Welcome, Sir Dominic. The cloakroom slave will furnish you with a mind-screen."

"What?" Despite himself, Flandry started.

"If you want one." Ruethen bared powerful teeth at Lady Diana. "Will my unknown friend grant me a dance later?"

She lost her own coolness for a second, then nodded graciously. "That would be a . . . unique experience, my lord," she said.

It would, at that. Flandry led her on into the ballroom. His mind worried Ruethen's curious offer, like a dog with a bone. Why?

He saw the gaunt black shape among the rainbow Terrans, and he knew. It went cold along his spine.

## CHAPTER II

HE WASTED no time on excuses, but almost ran to the cloakroom. His feet whispered along the crystalline floor, where Orion glittered hundreds of light-years beneath. "Mindscreen," he snapped.

The slave was a pretty girl. Merseians took pleasure in buying humans for menial jobs. "I've only a few, sir," she said. "His lordship told me to keep them for—"

"Me!" Flandry snatched the cap of wires, transistors, and power cells from her hesitant fingers. Only when it was on his head did he relax. Then he took out a fresh cigarette and steered through lilting music toward the bar. He needed a drink, badly.

Aycharaych of Chereion stood beneath high glass pillars. No one spoke to him. Most of the humans were dancing, while nonhumans of various races listened to the music. A performer from Lulluan spread heaven-blue feathers on a small stage, but few watched that rare sight. Flandry elbowed past a Merseian, who had just drained a two-liter tankard. "Scotch," he said. "Straight, tall, and quick."

Lady Diana approached. She seemed uncertain whether to be indignant or intrigued. "Now I know what they mean by cavalier treatment." She pointed upward. "What *is* that thing?"

Flandry tossed off his drink. The whiskey smoked down his throat, and he felt his nerves ease. "I'm told it's my face," he said.

"No, on! Stop fooling! I mean that horrible wire thing."

"Mind-screen." He held out his glass for a refill. "It heterodynes the energy radiation of the cerebral cortex in a random pattern. Makes it impossible to read what I'm thinking."

"But I thought that was impossible anyway," she said, bewildered. "I mean, unless you belong to a naturally telepathic species."

"Which man isn't," he agreed, "except for rare cases. The non-telepath develops his own private 'language,' which is gibberish to anyone who hasn't studied him for a long time as a single individual. Ergo, telepathy was never considered a particular threat in my line of work, and you've probably never heard of the mind-screen. It was developed just a few years ago. And the reason for its development is standing over there."

She followed his eyes. "Who? That tall being in the black mantle?"

"The same. I had a brush with him, and discovered to my—er—discomfiture, shall we say?—that he has a unique gift. Whether or not all his race does, I couldn't tell you. But within a range of a few hundred meters, Aycharaych of Chereion can read the mind of any individual of any species, whether he's ever met his victim before or not."

"But—why, then—!"

"Exactly. He's *persona non grata* throughout our territory, of course, to be shot on sight. But as you know, my lady," said Flandry in a bleak tone, "we are not now in the Terrestrial Empire. Jupiter belongs to the Dispersal of Ymir."

"Oh," said Lady Diana. She colored. "A telepath!"

Flandry gave her a lopsided grin. "Aycharaych is the equivalent of a gentleman," he said. "He wouldn't tell on you. But I'd better go talk to him now." He bowed. "You are certain not to lack company. I see a dozen men converging here already."

"So there are." She smiled. "But I think Aycharaych—how *do* you pronounce it, that guttural *oh* baffles me—I think he'll be much more intriguing." She took his arm.

Flandry disengaged her. She resisted. He closed a hand on her wrist and shoved it down with no effort. Maybe his visage was a fake, he told himself once in a while, but at least his body was his own, and the dreary hours of calisthenics had some reward. "I'm sorry, my lady," he said, "but I am about to talk shop, and you're not initiated in the second oldest profession. Have fun."

Her eyes flared offended vanity. She whirled about and welcomed the Duke of Mars with far more enthusiasm than that foolish young man warranted. Flandry sighed. *I suppose I owe you a thousand credits, Ivar.* He cocked his cigarette at a defiant angle, and strolled across the ballroom.

Aycharaych smiled. His face was also humanoid, but in a bony, sword-nosed fashion; the angles of mouth and jaw were exaggerated into V's. It might almost have been the face of some Byzantine saint. But the skin was a pure golden hue, the brows were arches of fine blue feathers, the bald skull carried a feather crest and pointed ears. Broad chest, wasp waist, long skinny legs were hidden by the cloak. The feet, with four clawed toes and spurs on the ankles, showed bare.

Flandry felt pretty sure that intelligent life on Chereion had evolved from birds, and that the planet must be dry, with a thin cold atmosphere. He had hints that its native civilization was incredibly old, and reason to believe it was not a mere subject of Merseia. But beyond that, his knowledge emptied into darkness. He didn't even know where in the

Merseian sphere the sun of Chereion lay.

Aycharaych extended a six-fingered hand. Flandry shook it. The digits were delicate within his own. For a brutal moment he thought of squeezing hard, crushing the fine bones. Aycharaych stood a bit taller than he, but Flandry was a rather big human, much broader and more solid.

"A pleasure to meet you again, Sir Dominic," said Aycharaych. His voice was low, sheer beauty to hear. Flandry looked at rust-red eyes, with a warm metallic luster, and released the hand.

"Hardly unexpected," he said. "For you, that is."

"You travel about so much," Aycharaych said. "I was sure a few men of your corps would be here tonight, but I could not be certain of your own whereabouts."

"I wish I ever was of yours," said Flandry ruefully.

"Congratulations upon your handling of *l'affaire Nyanza*. We are going to miss A'u on our side. He had a certain watery brilliance."

Flandry prevented himself from showing surprise. "I thought that aspect of the business had been hushed up," he said. "But little pitchers seem to have big ears. How long have you been in the Solar System?"

"A few weeks," said Aycharaych. "Chiefly a pleasure trip." He cocked his head. "Ah, the orchestra has begun a Strauss waltz. Very good. Though of course Johann is not to be compared to Richard, who will always be *the* Strauss."

"Oh?" Flandry's interest in ancient music was only slightly greater than his interest in committing suicide. "I wouldn't know."

"You should, my friend. Not even excepting Xingu, Strauss is the most misunderstood composer of known galactic history. Were I to be imprisoned for life with only one tape, I would choose his *Death and Transfiguration* and be satisfied."

"I'll arrange it," offered Flandry at once.

Archaraych chuckled and took the man's arm. "Come, let us find a more peaceful spot. But I pray you, do not waste so amusing an occasion on me. I own to visiting Terra clandestinely, but that part of it was entirely for the easement of my personal curiosity. I had no intention of burgling the Imperial offices—"

"Which are equipped with Aycharaych alarms anyway."

"Telepathizing detectors? Yes, so I would assume. I am a little too old and stiff, and your gravity a little too over-powering, to indulge in my own thefts. Nor have I the type of dashing good looks needed, I am told by all the teleplays, for cloak and dagger work. No, I merely wished to see the planet which bred such a race as yours. I walked in a few forests, inspected certain paintings, visited some chosen graves, and returned here. Whence I am about to depart, by the way. You need not get your Imperium to put pressure on the Ymirites to expel me; my courier ship leaves in twenty hours."

"For where?" asked Flandry.

"Hither and yon," said Aycharaych lightly.

Flandry felt his stomach muscles grow hard. "Syrax?" he got out.

They paused at the entrance to the null-gee conservatory. A single great sphere of water balanced like silver at its very heart with fern jungle and a thousand purple-scarlet blooms forming a cavern around it, the stars and mighty Jupiter beyond. Later, no doubt, the younger and drunker humans would be peeling off their clothes and going for a free-fall swim in that serene globe. But now only the music dwelt here. Aycharaych kicked himself over the threshold. His cloak flowed like black wings as he arrowed across the bubble-dome. Flandry came after, in clothes that were fire and trumpeting. He needed a moment before he adjusted to weightlessness. Aycharaych, whose ancestors once whistled in Chereion's sky, appeared to have no such trouble.

The nonhuman stopped his flight by seizing a bracken frond. He looked at a violet burst of orchids and his long hawk-head inclined. "Black against the quicksilver water globe," he mused, "the universe black and cold beyond both. A beautiful arrangement, and with that touch of horror necessary to the highest art."

"Black?" Flandry glanced startled at the violet flowers. Then he clamped his lips.

But Aycharaych had already grasped the man's idea. He smiled. "*Touché*. I should not have let slip that I am color-blind in the blue wave lengths."

"But you see further into the red than I do," predicted Flandry.

"Yes. I admit, since you would infer so anyhow, my native sun is cooler and redder than yours. If you think that will help you identify it, among all the millions of stars in the Merseian sphere, accept the information with my compliments."

"The Syrax Cluster is middle Population One," said Flandry. "Not too suitable for your eyes."

Aycharaych stared at the water. Tropical fish were visible within its globe, like tiny many-colored rockets. "It does not follow I am going to Syrax," he said tonelessly. "I certainly have no personal wish to do so. Too many warcraft, too many professional officers. I do not like their mentality." He made a free-fall bow. "Your own excepted, of course."

"Of course," said Flandry. "Still, if you could do something to break the deadlock out there, in Merseia's favor—"

"You flatter me," said Aycharaych. "But I fear you have not yet outgrown the romantic view of military politics. The fact is that neither side wants to make a total effort to control the Syrax stars. Merseia could use them as a valuable base, outflanking Antares and thus a spearhead poised at that entire sector of your empire. Terra wants control simply to deny us the cluster. Since neither government wishes, at present, to break the nominal state of peace, they maneuver about out there, mass naval strength, spy and snipe and hold running battles . . . but the game of all-out seizure is not worth the candle of all-out war."

"But if you could tip the scales, personally, so our boys lost out at Syrax," said Flandry, "we wouldn't counter attack your imperial sphere. You know that. It'd invite counter-counterattack on us. Heavens, Terra itself might be bombed! We're much too comfortable to risk such an outcome." He pulled himself up short. Why expose his own bitterness, and perhaps be arrested on Terra for sedition?

"If we possessed Syrax," said Aycharaych, "it would, with 71 percent probability, hasten the collapse of the Terran hegemony by a hundred years, plus or minus ten. That is the verdict of our military computers—though I myself feel the faith our High Command has in them is naive and rather touching. However, the predicted date of Terra's fall would still lie 150 years hence. So I wonder why your government cares."

Flandry shrugged. "A few of us are a bit sentimental about our planet," he answered sadly. "And then, of course, we ourselves aren't out there being shot at."

"That is the human mentality again," said Aycharaych. "Your instincts are such that you never accept dying. You, personally, underneath everything, do you not feel death is just a little bit vulgar, not quite a gentleman?"

"Maybe. What would you call it?"

"A completion."

Their talk drifted to impersonalities. Flandry had never found anyone else whom he could so converse with. Aycharaych could be wise and learned and infinitely kind when he chose; or flick a whetted wit across the pompous face of empire. To speak with him, touching now and then on the immortal questions, was almost like a confessional; for he was not human and did not judge human deeds, yet he seemed to understand the wishes at their root.

At last Flandry made a reluctant excuse to get away. *Nu,* he told himself, *business is business.* Since Lady Diana was studiously ignoring him, he enticed a red-haired bit of fluff into an offside room, told her he would be back in ten minutes, and slipped through a rear corridor. Perhaps any Merseian who saw him thus disappear wouldn't expect him to return for an hour or two; might not recognize the girl when she got bored waiting and found her own way to the ballroom again. One human looked much like another to the untrained nonhuman eye, and there were at least a thousand guests by now.

It was a flimsy camouflage for his exit, but the best he could think of.

Flandry re-entered the yacht and roused Chives. "Home," he said. "Full acceleration. Or secondary drive, if you think you can handle it within the System in this clumsy gold-plated hulk."

"Yes, sir. I can."

At faster-than-light, he'd be at Terra in minutes, rather than hours. Excellent! It might actually be possible to arrange for Aycharaych's completion.

More than half of Flandry hoped the attempt would fail.

## CHAPTER III

IT HAPPENED to be day over North America, where Vice Admiral Fenross had his offices. Not that that mattered; they were like as not to work around the clock in Intelligence, or else Flandry could have gotten his superior out of bed. He would, in fact, have preferred to do so.

As matters worked out, however, he created a satisfactory commotion. He saved an hour by having Chives dive the yacht illegally through all traffic lanes above Admiralty Center. With a coverall over his party clothes, he dove from the airlock and rode a grav repulser down to the 40th flange of the Intelligence tower. While the yacht was being stopped by a sky monitor, Flandry was arguing with a marine on guard duty. He looked down the muzzle of a blaster and said, "You know me, sergeant. Let me by. Urgent."

"I guess I do know your face, sir," the marine answered. "But faces can be changed and nobody gets by me without a pass. Just stand there while I buzzes a patrol."

Flandry considered making a jump for it. But the Imperial Marines were on to every trick of judo he knew. Hell take it, an hour wasted on identification! Wait. Memory clicked into place. "You're Mohandas Parkinson," said Flandry. "You have four darling children, your wife is unreasonably monogamous, and you were playing Go at Madam Cepheid's last month."

Sergeant Parkinson's gun wavered. "Huh?" he said, Then, loudly, "I don' know whatcher talking about!"

"Madame Cepheid's Go board is twenty meters square," said Flandry, "and the pieces are live girls. In the course of a game— Does that ring a bell, sergeant? I was there too, watching, and I'm sure your wife would be delighted to hear you are still capable of such truly epic—"

"Get on your way, you . . . blackmailer!" choked Parkinson. He gulped and added, "Sir."

Captain Flandry grinned, patted him on his helmet, holstered his weapon for him, and went quickly inside.

Unlike most, Fenross had no beautiful receptionist in his outer office. A robovoice asked the newcomer's business. "Hero," he said blandly. The robot said Admiral Fenross was occupied with a most disturbing new development. Flandry said he was also, and got admission.

Hollow-cheeked and shaky, Fenross looked across his desk. His eyes were not too bloodshot to show a flick of hatred. "Oh," he said. "You. Well, Captain, what interrupts your little *tete-a-tete* with your Merseian friends?"

Flandry sat down and took out a cigarette. He was not surprised that Fenross had set spies on him, but the fact was irritating nonetheless. *How the devil did this feud ever get started?* he wondered. *Is it only that I took that girl . . . what was her name anyway? Marjorie? Margaret? . . . was it only that I once took her from him when we were cadets together? Why, I did it for a joke. She wasn't very good-looking, in spite of everything biosculp could do.*

"I've news too hot for any com circuit," he said. "I just now—"

"You're on furlough," snapped Fenross. "You've got no business here."

"What? Look, it was Aycharaych! Himself! At the Crystal Moon!"

A muscle twitched in Fenross' cheek. "I can't hear an unofficial report," he said. "All ruin is exploding beyond Aldebaran. If you think you've done something brilliant, file an account in the regular channels."

"But—for God's sake!" Flandry sprang to his feet. "Admiral Fenross, sir, whatever the hell you want me to call you, he's leaving the Solar System in a matter of hours. Courier boat. We can't touch him in Ymirite space, but if we waylaid him on his way out. He'll be tricky, the ambush might not work, but name of a little green pig, if we can get Aycharaych it'll be better than destroying a Merseian fleet!"

Fenross reached out a hand which trembled ever so faintly, took a small pillbox and shook a tablet loose. "Haven't slept in forty hours," he muttered. "And you off on that yacht. . . . I can't take cognizance, Captain. Not under the circumstances." He glanced up again. Slyness glistened in his eyes. "Of course," he said, "if you want to cancel your own leave—"

Flandry stood a moment, rigid, staring at the desk-bound man who hated him. Memory trickled back: *After I broke off with her, yes, the girl did go a bit wild. She was killed in an accident on Venus, wasn't she . . . drunken party flying over the Saw . . . yes, I seem to've heard about it. And Fenross has never even looked at another woman.*

He sighed. "Sir, I am reporting myself back on active duty."

Fenross nodded. "File that with the robot as you leave. Now I've got work for you."

"But Aycharaych—"

"We'll handle him. I've got a more suitable assignment in mind." Fenross grinned, tossed down his pill and followed it with a cup of water from the desk fountain. "After all, a dashing field agent ought to dash, don't you think?"

*Could it be just the fact that he's gotten more rank but*

*I've had more fun?* wondered Flandry. *Who knows? Does he himself?* He sat down again, refusing to show expression.

Fenross drummed the desk top and stared at a blank wall. His uniform was as severe as regulations permitted—Flandry's went in the opposite direction—but it still formed an unnecessarily gorgeous base for his tortured red head. "This is under the strictest secrecy," he began in a rapid, toneless voice. "I have no idea how long we can suppress the news, though. One of our colonies is under siege. Deep within the Imperial sphere."

Flandry was forced to whistle. "Where? Who?"

"Ever heard of Vixen? Well, I never had, either, before this. It's a human-settled planet of an F6 star about a hundred light-years from Sol, somewhat north and clockwise of Aldebaran. Odd ball world, but moderately successful as colonies go. You know that region is poor in systems of interest to humans, and very little explored. In effect, Vixen sits in the middle of a desert. Or does it? You'll wonder when I tell you that a space fleet appeared several weeks ago and demanded that it yield to occupation. The ships were of exotic type, and the race crewing them can't be identified. But some, at least, spoke pretty good Anglic."

Flandry sat dead still. His mind threw up facts, so familiar as to be ridiculous, and yet they must now be considered again. The thing which had happened was without precedent.

An interstellar domain can have no definite borders; stars are scattered too thinly, their types too intermingled. And there are too many of them. In very crude approximation, the Terrestrial Empire was a sphere of some 400 light-years diameter, centered on Sol, and contained an estimated four million stars. But of these less than half had ever been visited. A bare 100,000 were directly concerned with the Imperium, a few multiples of that number might have some shadowy contact and owe a theoretical allegiance. Consider a single planet; realize that it is a *world,* as big and varied and strange as this Terra ever was, with as many conflicting elements of race and language and culture among its natives; estimate how much government even one planet requires, and see how quickly a reign over many becomes impossibly huge. Then consider, too, how small a percentage of stars are of any use to a given species (too hot, too cold, too turbulent, too many companions) and, of those, how few will have even one planet where that species is reasonably safe. The Empire becomes tenuous indeed. And its inconceivable extent is still the merest speck in one outlying part of one spiral arm of one galaxy; among a hundred billion or more great suns, those known to any single world are the barest, tiniest handful.

However—attack that far within the sphere? No! Individual ships could sneak between the stars easily enough. But a war fleet could never come a hundred light-years inward from the farthest Imperial bases. The instantaneous "wake" of disturbed space time, surging from so many vessels, would be certain of detection somewhere along the line. Therefore—

"Those ships were built within our sphere," said Flandry slowly. "And not too many parsecs from Vixen."

Fenross sneered. "Your genius dazzles me. As a matter of fact, though, they might have come further than usual, undetected, because so much of the Navy is out at Syrax now. Our interior posts are stripped, some completely deserted. I'll agree the enemy must base within several parsecs of Vixen. But that doesn't mean they live there. Their base might be a space station, a rogue planet, or something else we'll never find; they could have sent their fleet to it a ship at a time, over a period of months."

Flandry shook his head. "Supply lines. Having occupied Vixen, they'll need to maintain their garrison till it's self-sufficient. No, they have a home somewhere in the Imperial sphere, surely in the same quadrant. Which includes only about a million stars! Say, roughly, 100,000 possibilities, some never even catalogued. How many years would it take how many ships to check out 100,000 systems?"

"Yeh. And what would be happening meanwhile?"

"What has?"

"The Vixenites put up a fight. There's a small naval base on their planet, unmanned at present, but enough of the civilian population knew how to make use of its arsenal. They got couriers away, of course, and Aldebaran Station sent what little help it could. When last heard from, Vixen was under seige. We're dispatching a task force, but it'll take time to get there. That wretched Syrax business ties our hands. Reports indicate the aliens haven't overwhelming strength; we could send enough ships to make mesons of them. But if we withdrew that many from Syrax, they'd come back to find Merseia entrenched in the Cluster."

"Tie-in?" wondered Flandry.

"Who knows? I've got an idea, though, and your assignment will be to investigate it." Fenross leaned over the desk. His sunken eyes probed at Flandry's. "We're all too ready to think of Merseia when anything goes wrong," he said bleakly. "But after all, they live a long ways off. There's another alien power right next door . . . and as closely interwoven with Merseia as it is with us."

"You mean Ymir?" Flandry snorted. "Come now, dear chief, you're letting your xenophobia run away with you."

"Consider," said Fenross. "Somebody, or something, helped those aliens at Vixen build a modern war fleet. They couldn't have done it alone; we'd have known it if they'd begun exploring stellar space, and knowledge has to precede conquest. Somebody, very familiar with our situation, has briefed the aliens on our language, weapons, territorial layout—the works. Somebody, I'm sure, told them when to attack; right now, when nearly our whole strength is at Syrax. *Who*? There's one item. The aliens use a helium-pressure power system like the Ymirites. That's unmistakable on the detectors. Helium-pressure is all right, but it's not as convenient as the hydrogen-heavy atom cycle; not if you live under terrestroid conditions, and the aliens very definitely do. The ships, their shape I mean, also have a subtly Ymirite touch. I'll show you pictures that have arrived with the reports. Those ships look as if they'd been designed by some engineer more used to working with hydrolithium than steel.."

"You mean the Ymirites are behind the aliens? But—"

"But nothing. There's an Ymirite planet in the Vixen

system too. Who knows how many stars those crawlers have colonized . . . stars we never even heard about? Who knows how many client races they might lord it over? And they travel blithely back and fourth, across our sphere and Merseia's and—Suppose they are secretly in cahoots with Merseia. What better way to smuggle Merseian agents into our systems? We don't stop Ymirite ships. We aren't able to! But any of them could carry a force-bubble with terrestroid conditions inside. . . . I've felt for years we've been too childishly trustful of Ymir. It's past time we investigated them in detail. It may already be too late!"

Flandry stubbed out his cigarette. "But what interest have they got in all this?" he asked mildly. "What could any oxygen-breathing race have that they'd covet—or bribe them with?"

"That I don't know," said Fenross. "I could be dead wrong. But I want it looked into. You're going back to Jupiter, Captain. At once."

"What?"

"We're chronically undermanned in this miserable step-child of the service," said Fenross. "Now, worse than ever. You'll have to go alone. Snoop around as much as you can. Take all the time you need. But don't come back without a report that'll give some indication—one way or another!"

*Or come back dead,* thought Flandry. He looked into the twitching face across the desk and knew that was what Fenross wanted.

# CHAPTER IV

HE GOT CHIVES out of arrest and debated with himself whether to sneak back to Ruethen's party. It was still going on. But no. Aycharaych would never have mentioned his own departure without assuming Flandry would notify headquarters. It might be his idea of a joke—it might be a straightforward challenge, for Aycharaych was just the sort who'd enjoy seeing if he could elude an ambush—most likely, the whole thing was deliberate, for some darkling purpose. In any event, a junior Intelligence officer or two could better keep tabs on the Chereionite than the too well-known Flandry. Having made arrangements for that the man took Chives to his private flitter.

Though voluptuous enough inside, the *Hooligan* was a combat boat, with guns and speed. Even on primary, sub-light drive, it could reach Jupiter in so few hours that Flandry would have little enough time to think what he would do. He set the autopilot and bade Chives bring a drink. "A stiff one," he added.

"Yes, sir. Do you wish your whites laid out, or do you prefer a working suit?"

Flandry considered his rumpled elegance and sighed. Chives had spent an hour dressing him—for nothing. "Plain gray zipsuit," he said. "Also sackcloth and ashes."

"Very good, sir." The valet poured whiskey over ice. He was from Shalmu, quite humanoid except for bald emerald skin, prehensile tail, one-point-four meter height, and details

23

of ear, hand, and foot. Flandry had bought him some years back, named him Chives, and taught him any number of useful arts. Lately, the being had politely refused freedom. ("If I may make so bold as to say it, sir, I am afraid my tribal customs would now have a lack of interest for me matched only by their deplorable lack of propriety.")

Flandry brooded over his drink a while. "What do you know about Ymir?" he asked.

"Ymir is the arbitrary human name, sir, for the chief planet of a realm—if I may use that word advisedly—coterminous with the Terrestrial Empire, the Merseian, and doubtless a considerable part of the galaxy beyond."

"Don't be so bloody literal-minded," said Flandry. "Especially when I'm being rhetorical. I mean, what do you know about their ways of living, thinking, believing, hoping? What do they find beautiful and what is too horrible to tolerate? Good galloping gods, what do they even use for a government? They call themselves the Dispersal when they talk Anglic; but is that a translation or a mere tag? How can we tell? What do you and I have in common with a being that lives at a hundred below zero, breathing hydrogen at a pressure which makes our ocean beds look like vacuum, drinking liquid methane and using allotropic ice to make his tools?

"We were ready enough to cede Jupiter to them; Jupiter-type planets throughout our realm. They had terrestroid planets to offer in exchange. Why, that swap doubled the volume of our sphere. And we traded a certain amount of scientific information with them, high-pressure physics for low-pressure, oxygen metabolisms versus hydrogen . . . but disappointingly little, when you get down to it. They'd been in interstellar space longer than we had. (And how did they learn atomics under Ymirite air pressure? We don't ask it!) They'd already observed our kind of life throughout . . . how much of the galaxy? We couldn't offer them a thing of importance, except the right to colonize some more planets in peace. They've never shown as much interest in our wars—the wars of the oxygen breathers on the pygmy planets— as you and I would have in a fight between two ant armies. Why should they care? You could drop Terra or Merseia into Jupiter and it'd hardly make a decent splash. For a hundred years, now, the Ymirites have scarcely said a word to us. Or to Merseia, from all indications. Till now.

"And yet I glanced at the pictures taken out near Vixen, just before we left. And Fenross, may he fry, is right. Those blunt ships were made on a planet similar to Terra, but they have Ymirite lines . . . the way the first Terran automobiles had the motor in front, because that was where the horse used to be. . . . It could be coincidence, I suppose. Or a red herring. Or—I don't know. How am I supposed to find out, one man on a planet with ten times the radius of Terra? Judas!" He drained his glass and held it out again.

Chives refilled, then went back to the clothes locker. "A white scarf or a blue?" he mused. "Hm, yes, I do believe the white, sir."

The flitter plunged onward. Flandry needed a sober jolt by the time he had landed on Ganymede.

There was an established procedure for such a visit. It hadn't been used for decades, Flandry had had to look it up, but the robot station still waited patiently between rough mountains. He presented his credentials, radio contact was made with the primary planet, unknown messages traveled over its surface. A reply was quick: yes, Captain, the governor can receive you. A spaceship is on its way, and will be at your disposal.

Flandry looked out at the stony desolation of Ganymede. It was not long before a squat, shimmering shape had made grav-beam descent. A tube wormed from its lock to the flitter's. Flandry sighed. "Let's go," he said, and strolled across. Chives trotted after with a burden of weapons, tools, and instruments—none of which were likely to be much use. There was a queasy moment under Ganymede's natural gravity, then they had entered the Terra-conditioned bubble.

It looked like any third-class passenger cabin, except for the outmoded furnishings and a bank of large viewscreens. Hard to believe that this was only the material inner lining of a binding-force field; that that same energy, cousin to that which held the atomic nucleus together, was all which kept this room from being crushed beneath intolerable pressure. Or, at the moment, kept the rest of the spaceship from exploding outward. The bulk of the vessel was an alloy of water, lithium, and metallic hydrogen, stable only under Jovian surface conditions.

Flandry let Chives close the air lock while he turned on the screens. They gave him a full outside view. One remained blank, a communicator, the other showed the pilot's cabin.

An artificial voice, ludicrously sweet in the style of a century ago, said, "Greeting, Terran. My name, as nearly as it may be rendered in sonic equivalents, is Horx. I am your guide and interpreter while you remain on Jupiter."

Flandry looked into the screen. The Ymirite didn't quite register on his mind. His eyes weren't trained to those shapes and proportions, seen by that weirdly shifting red-blue-brassy light. (Which wasn't the real thing, even, but an electronic translation. A human looking straight into the thick Jovian air would only see darkness.) "Hello, Horx," he said to the great black multi-legged shape with the peculiarly tendrilled heads. He wet his lips, which seemed a bit dry. "I, er, expect you haven't had such an assignment before in your life."

"I did several times, a hundred or so Terra-years ago," said Horx casually. He didn't seem to move, to touch any controls, but Ganymede receded in the viewscreens and raw space blazed forth. "Since then I have been doing other work." Hesitation. Or was it? At last, "Recently, though, I have conducted several missions to our surface."

"What?" choked Flandry.

"Merseian," said Horx. "You may inquire of the governor if you wish." He said nothing else the whole trip.

Jupiter, already big in the scene, became half of heaven. Flandry saw blots march across its glowing many-colored face, darknesses which were storms that could have swallowed all Terra. Then the sight was lost, he was dropping through the atmosphere. Still the step-up screens tried loyally to show him something; he saw clouds of ammonia crystals, a thousand kilometers long, streaked with strange blues and greens that were free radicals; he saw lightning leap across a purple sky, and the distant yellow flare of sodium explosions. As he descended, he could even feel, very dimly, the quiver of the ship under enormous winds, and hear the muffled shriek and thunder of the air.

They circled the night side, still descending, and Flandry saw a methane ocean, beating waves flattened by pressure and gravity against a cliff of black allotropic ice, which crumbled and was lifted again even as he watched. He saw an endless plain where things half trees and half animals— except that they were neither, in any Terrestrial sense— lashed snaky fronds after ribbon-shaped flyers a hundred meters in length. He saw bubbles stream past on a red wind, and they were lovely in their myriad colors and they sang in thin crystal voices which somehow penetrated the ship. But they couldn't be true bubbles at this pressure. Could they?

A city came into view, just beyond the dawn line. If it was a city. It was, at least, a unified structure of immense extent, intricate with grottos and arabesques, built low throughout, but somehow graceful and gracious. On Flandry's screen its color was polished blue. Here and there sparks and threads of white energy would briefly flash. They hurt his eyes. There were many Ymirites about, flying on their own wings or riding in shell-shaped power gliders. You wouldn't think of Jupiter as a planet where anything could fly, until you remembered the air density; then you realized it was more a case of swimming.

The spaceship came to a halt, hovering on its repulsor field. Horx said, "Governor Thua."

Another Ymirite squatted suddenly in the outside communication screen. He held something which smoked and flickered from shape to shape. The impersonally melodious robot voice said for him, under the eternal snarling of a wind which would have blown down any city men could build, "Welcome. What is your desire?"

The old records had told Flandry to expect brusqueness. It was not discourtesy; what could a human and an Ymirite make small talk about? The man puffed a cigarette to nervous life and said, "I am here on an investigative mission for my government." Either these beings were or were not already aware of the Vixen situation; if not, then they weren't allies of Merseia and would presumably not tell. Or if they did, what the devil difference? Flandry explained.

Thua said at once, "You seem to have very small grounds for suspecting us. A mere similarity of appearances and nuclear technology is logically insufficient."

"I know," said Flandry. "It could be a fake."

"It could even be that one or a few Ymirite individuals have offered advice to the entities which instigated this attack," said Thua. You couldn't judge from the pseudo-voice, but he seemed neither offended nor sympathetic; just monumentally uninterested. "The Dispersal has been nonstimulate as regards individuals for many cycles. However, I cannot imagine what motive an Ymirite would have for exerting himself on behalf of oxygen breathers. There is no insight to be gained from such acts, and certainly no material profit."

"An aberrated individual?" suggested Flandry with little hope. "Like a man poking an anthill—an abode of lesser animals—merely to pass the time?"

"Ymirites do not aberrate in such fashion," said Thua stiffly.

"I understand there've been recent Merseian visits here."

"I was about to mention that. I am doing all I can to assure both empires of Ymir's strict neutrality. It would be a nuisance if either attacked us and forced us to exterminate their species."

*Which is the biggest brag since that fisherman who caught the equator,* thought Flandry, *or else is sober truth.* He said aloud, choosing his words one by one, "What, then, were the Merseians doing here?"

"They wished to make some scientific observations of the Jovian surface," said Thua. "Horx guided them, like you. Let him describe their activities."

The pilot stirred in his chamber, spreading black wings. "We simply cruised about a few times. They had optical instruments, and took various spectroscopic readings. They said it was for research in solid-state physics."

"Curiouser and curiouser," said Flandry. He stroked his mustache. "They have as many Jovoid planets in their sphere as we do. The detailed report on Jovian conditions which the first Ymirite settlers made to Terra, under the treaty, has never been secret. No, I just don't believe that research yarn."

"It did seem dubious," agreed Thua, "but I do not pretend to understand every vagary of the alien mind. It was easier to oblige them than argue about it."

Chives cleared his throat and said unexpectedly, "If I may take the liberty of a question, sir, were all these recent visitors of the Merseian species?"

Thua's disgust could hardly be mistaken, "Do you expect me to register insignificant differences between one such race and another?"

Flandry sighed. "It looks like deadlock, doesn't it?" he said.

"I can think of no way to give you positive assurance that Ymir is not concerned, except my word," said Thua. "However, if you wish, you may cruise about this planet at random and see if you observe anything out of the ordinary." His screen went blank.

"Big fat chance!" muttered Flandry. "Give me a drink, Chives."

"Will you follow the governor's proposal?" asked Horx.

"Reckon so." Flandry flopped into a chair. "Give us the standard guided tour. I've never been on Jupiter, and might as well have something to show for my time."

The city fell behind, astonishingly fast. Flandry sipped the whiskey Chives had gotten from the supplies they had along, and watched the awesome landscape with half an eye. Too bad he was feeling so sour; this really was an experience such as is granted few men. But he had wasted hours on a mission which any second-year cadet could have handled . . . while guns were gathered at Syrax and Vixen stood alone against all hell . . . or even while Lady Diana danced with other men and Ivar del Bruno waited grinning to collect his bet. Flandry said an improper word. "What a nice subtle bed of coals for Fenross to rake me over," he added. "The man has a genius for it." He gulped his drink and called for another.

"We're rising, sir," said Chives much later.

Flandry saw mountains which trembled and droned, blue mists that whirled about their metallic peaks, and then the Jovian ground was lost in darkness. The sky began to turn blood color. "What are we heading for now?" he asked. He checked a map. "Oh, yes, I see."

"I venture to suggest to the pilot, sir, that our speed may be a trifle excessive," said Chives.

Flandry heard the wind outside rise to a scream, with subsonic undertones that shivered in his marrow. Red fog flew roiled and tattered past his eyes. Beyond, he saw crimson clouds the height of a Terrestrial sierra, with lightning leaping in their bellies. The light from the screens washed like a dull fire into the cabin.

"Yes," he muttered. "Slow down, Horx. There'll be another one along in a minute, as the story has it—"

And then he saw the pilot rise up in his chamber, fling open a door, and depart. An instant afterward Flandry saw Horx beat wings against the spaceship's furious slipstream; then the Ymirite was whirled from view. And then Chives saw the thing which hung in the sky before them, and yelled. He threw his tail around Flandry's waist while he clung with hands and legs to a bunk stanchion.

And then the world exploded into thunder and night.

## CHAPTER V

FLANDRY awoke. He spent centuries wishing he hadn't. A blurred green shape said: "You aneurine, sir."

"Go 'way," mumbled Flandry. "What was I drinking?"

"Pardon my taking the liberty, sir," said Chives. He pinned the man's wrists down with his tail, held Flandry's nose with one hand and poured the drug down his mouth with the other. "There, now, we are feeling much better, aren't we?"

"Remind me to shoot you, slowly." Flandry gagged for a while. The medicine took hold and he sat up. His brain cleared and he looked at the screen bank.

Only one of the viewers still functioned. It showed thick, drifting redness, shot through with blues and blacks. A steady rough growling, like the breakup of a polar ice pack, blasted its way through the ultimate rigidity of the force bubble. God, what must the noise be like outside? The cabin was tilted. Slumped in its lower corner, Flandry began to glide across the floor again; the ship was still being rolled about. The internal gravity field had saved their lives by cushioning the worst shock, but then it had gone dead. He felt the natural pull of Jupiter upon him, and every cell was weary from its own weight.

He focused on a twisted bunkframe. "Did I do that with my own little head?"

"We struck with great force, sir," Chives told him. "I permitted myself to bandage your scalp. However, a shot of growth hormone will heal the cuts in a few hours, sir, if we escape the present dilemma."

31

Flandry lurched to his feet. His bones seemed to be dragging him back downward. He felt the cabin walls tremble and heard them groan. The force bubble had held, which meant that its generator and the main power plant had survived the crash. Not unexpectedly; a ship like this was built on the "fail safe" principle. But there was no access whatsoever from this cabin to the pilot room—·unless you were an Ymirite. It made no difference whether the ship was still flyable or not. Human and Shalmuan were stuck here till they starved. Or, more likely, till the atomic-power plant quit working, under the buffets this ship was receiving.

Well, when the force-field collapsed and Jovian air pressure flattened the cabin, it would be a merciful death.

"The hell with that noise," said Flandry. "I don't want to die so fast I can't feel it. I want to see death coming, and make the stupid thing fight for every centimeter of me."

"Chives gazed into the sinister crimson which filled the last electronic window. His slight frame stooped, shaking in the knees; he was even less adapted to Jovian weight than Flandry. "Where are we, sir?" he husked. "I was thinking primarily about what to make for lunch, just before the collision, and—"

"The Red Spot area," said Flandry. "Or, rather, the fringe of it. We must be on an outlying berg, or whatever the deuce they're called."

"Our guide appears to have abandoned us, sir."

"Hell, he got us into this mess. On purpose! I now know for a fact there's at least one Ymirite working for the enemy—whoever the enemy is. But the information won't be much use if we become a pair of grease spots."

The ship shuddered and canted. Flandry grabbed a stanchion for support, eased himself down on the bunk, and said, very quickly, for destruction roared around him, "You've seen the Red Spot from space, Chives. It's been known for a long time, even before space travel, that it's a . . . a mass of aerial pack ice. Lord, what a fantastic place to die! What happens is that at a certain height in the Jovian atmosphere, the pressure allows a red crystalline form on ice—not the

white stuff we splash whiskey onto, or the black allotrope
down at the surface, or the super-dense variety in the mantle
around the Jovian core. Here the pressure is right for red
ice, and the air density is identical, so it floats. An initial
formation created favorable conditions for the formation of
more . . . so it accumulated in this one region, much as
polar caps build up on cozier type planets. Some years a lot
of it melts away—changes phase—the Red Spot looks paler
from outside. Other years you get a heavy pile-up, and Jupiter
seems to have a moving wound. But always, Chives, the Red
Spot is a pack of flying glaciers, stretching broader than all
Terra. And we've been crashed on one of them!"

"Then our present situation can scarcely be accidental,
sir," nodded Chives imperturbably. "I daresay, with all
the safety precautions built into this ship, Horx thought
this would be the only way to destroy us without leaving
evidence. He can claim a stray berg was tossed in our path,
or some such tale." Chives sniffed. "Not sportsmanlike at
all, sir. Just what one would expect of a . . . a native."

The cabin yawed. Flandry caught himself before he fell
out of the bunk. At this gravity, to stumble across the room
would be to break a leg. Thunders rolled. White vapors
hissed up against crimson in the surviving screen.

"I'm not on to these scientific esoterica," said Flandry.
His chest pumped, struggling to supply oxygen for muscles
toiling under nearly three times their normal weight. Each
rib felt as if cast in lead. "But I'd guess what is happening
is this. We maintain a temperature in here which for Jupiter
is crazily high. So we're radiating heat, which makes the
ice go soft and—we're slowly sinking into the berg." He
shrugged and got out a cigarette.

"Is that wise, sir?" asked Chives.

"The oxygen recyclers are still working," said Flandry. "It's
not at all stuffy in here. Air is the least of our worries." His
cooiness cracked over, he smote a fist on the wall and said
between his teeth, "It's this being helpless! We can't go out
of the cabin, we can't do a thing but sit here and take it!"

"I wonder, sir." Slowly, his thin face sagging with gravity,

Chives pulled himself to the pack of equipment. He pawed through it. "No, sir. I regret to say I took no radio. It seemed we could communicate through the pilot." He paused. "Even if we did find a way to signal, I daresay any Ymirite who received our call would merely interpret it as random static."

Flandry stood up, somehow. "What do we have?" A tiny excitement shivered along his nerves. Outside, Jupiter boomed at him.

"Various detectors, sir, to check for installations. A pair of spacesuits. Sidearms. Your burglar kit, though I confess uncertainty what value it would have here. A microrecorder. A—"

*"Wait a minute!"*

Flandry sprang toward his valet. The floor rocked beneath him. He staggered toward the far wall. Chives shot out his tail and helped brake the man. Shaking, Flandry eased himself down and went on all fours to the corner where the Shalmuan squatted.

He didn't even stop to gibe at his own absent-mindedness. His heart thuttered. "Wait a minute, Chives," he said. "We've got an airlock over there. Since the force-bubble necessarily reinforces its structure, it must still be intact; and its machinery can open the valves even against this outside pressure. Of course, we can't go through ourselves. Our space armor would be squashed flat. But we can get at the mechanism of the lock. It also, by logical necessity, has to be part of the Terra-conditioned system. We can use the tools we have here to make a simple automatic cycle. First the outer valve opens. Then it shuts, the Jovian air is exhausted from the chamber and Terrestrial air replaces same. Then the valve opens again . . . and so on. Do you see?"

"No, sir," said Chives. A deadly physical exhaustion filmed his yellow eyes. "My brain feels so thick . . . I regret—"

"A signal!" yelled Flandry. "We flush oxygen out into a hydrogencum-methane atmosphere. We supply an electric spark in the lock chamber to ignite the mixture. Whoosh! A flare! Feeble and blue enough—but not by Jovian standards. Any Ymirite anywhere within tens of kilometers is bound to see it as brilliant as we see a magnesium torch. And it'll repeat. A steady cycle, every four or five minutes. If the Ymirites aren't made of concrete, they'll be curious enough to investigate . . . and when they find the wreck on this berg, they'll guess our need and—"

His voice trailed off. Chives said dully, "Can we spare the oxygen, sir?"

"We'll have to," said Flandry. "We'll sacrifice as much as we can stand, and then halt the cycle. If nothing has happened after several hours, we'll expend half of what's left in one last fire works." He took an ultimate pull on his cigarette, ground it out with great care, and fought back to his feet. "Come on, let's get going. What have we to lose?"

The floor shook. It banged and crashed outside. A fog of free radicals drifted green past the window, and the red iceberg spun in Jupiter's endless gale.

Flandry glanced at Chives. "You have one fault, laddy," he said, forcing a smile to his lips. "You aren't a beautiful woman." And then, after a moment, sighing, "However, it's just as well. Under the circumstances."

## CHAPTER VI

AND IN *that well-worn nick of time, which goes to prove that the gods, understandably, love me, help arrived. An Ymirite party spotted our flare. Having poked around, they went off, bringing back another force-bubble ship to which we transferred our nearly suffocated carcasses. No, Junior, I don't know what the Ymirites were doing in the Red Spot area. It must be a dank cold place for them, too. But I had guessed they would be sure to maintain some kind of monitors, scientific stations, or what have you around there, just as we monitor the weather-breeding regions of Terra.*

*Governor Thua didn't bother to apologize. He didn't even notice my valet's indignant demand that the miscreant Horx be forthwith administered a red-ice shaft, except to say that future visitors would be given a different guide (how can they tell?) and that this business was none of his doing and he wouldn't waste any Ymirite's time with investigations or punishments or any further action at all. He pointed out the treaty provision, that he wasn't bound to admit us, and that any visits would always be at the visitor's own risk.*

*The fact that some Ymirites did rescue us proves that the conspiracy, if any, does not involve their whole race. But how highly placed the hostile individuals are in their government (if they have anything corresponding to government as we know it) I haven't the groggiest.*

*Above summary for convenience only. Transcript of all conversation, which was taped as per ungentlemanly orders, attached.*

*Yes, Junior, you may leave the room.*

Flandry switched off the recorder. He could trust the confidential secretary, who would make a formal report out of his dictation, to clean it up. Though he wished she wouldn't.

He leaned back, cocked feet on desk, trickled smoke through his nostrils, and looked out the clear wall of his office. Admiralty Center gleamed, slim faerie spires in soft colors, reaching for the bright springtime sky of Terra. You couldn't mount guard across 400 light-years without millions of ships; and that meant millions of policy makers, scientists, strategists, tacticians, co-ordinators, clerks . . . and they had families, which needed food, clothing, houses, schools, amusements . . . so the heart of the Imperial Navy became a city in its own right. *Damn company town,* thought Flandry. And yet, when the bombs finally roared out of space, when the barbarians howled among smashed buildings and the smoke of burning books hid dead men in tattered bright uniforms—

when the Long Night came, as it would a century or a millennium hence, what difference?—something of beauty and gallantry would have departed the universe.

To hell with it. Let civilization hang together long enough for Dominic Flandry to taste a few more vintages, ride a few more horses, kiss a lot more girls and sing another ballad or two. That would suffice. At least, it was all he dared hope for.

The intercom chimed. "Admiral Fenross wants to see you immediately, sir."

"Now he tells me," grunted Flandry. "I wanted to see him yesterday, when I got back."

"He was busy then, sir," said the robot, as glibly as if it had a conscious mind. "His lordship the Earl of Sidrath is visiting Terra, and wished to be conducted through the operations center."

Flandry rose, adjusted his peacock-blue tunic, admired the crease of his gold-frogged white trousers, and covered his sleek hair with a jewel-banded officer's cap. "Of course," he said, "Admiral Fenross couldn't possibly delegate the tour to an aide."

"The Earl of Sidrath is related to Grand Admiral the Duke of Asia," the robot reminded him.

Flandry sang beneath his breath, *"Brown is the color of my true love's nose,"* and went out the door. After a series of slideways and gravshafts, he reached Fenross' office.

The admiral nodded his close-cropped head beyond the desk. "There you are." His tone implied Flandry had stopped for a beer on the way. "Sit down. Your preliminary verbal report on the Jovian mission has been communicated to me. Is that really all you could find out?"

Flandry smiled. "You told me to get an indication, one way or another, of the Ymirite attitude, sir," he purred. "That's what I got; an indication, one way or another."

Fenross gnawed his lip. "All right, all right. I should have known, I guess. Your forte never was working with an organization, and we're going to need a special project, a very large project, to learn the truth about Ymir."

Flandry sat up straight. "Don't," he said sharply.

"What?"

"Don't waste men that way. Sheer arithmetic will defeat them. Jupiter alone has the area of a hundred Terras. The population must be more or less proportional. How are our men going to percolate around, confined to the two or three spaceships that Thua has available for them? Assuming Thua doesn't simply refuse to admit any further oxygen-breathing nuisances. How are they going to question, bribe, eavesdrop, get any single piece of information? It's a truism that the typical Intelligence job consists of gathering a million unimportant little facts and fitting them together into one big fact. We've few enough agents as is, spread ghastly thin. Don't tie them up in an impossible job. Let them keep working on Merseia, where they've a chance of accomplishing something!"

"And if Ymir suddenly turns on us?" snapped Fenross.

"Then we roll with the punch. Or we die." Flandry shrugged and winced; his muscles were still sore from the pounding they had taken. "But haven't you thought, sir, this whole business may well be a Merseian stunt—to divert our attention from them, right at this crisis? It's exactly the sort of bear trap Aycharaych loves to set."

"That may be," admitted Fenross. "But Merseia lies beyond Syrax; Jupiter is next door. I've been given to understand that His Imperial Majesty is alarmed enough to desire—" He shrugged too, making it the immemorial gesture of a baffled underling.

"Who dropped that hint?" drawled Flandry. "Surely not the Earl of Sidrath, whom you were showing the sights yesterday while the news came in that Vixen had fallen?"

"Shut up!" Almost, it was a scream. A jag of pain went over Fenross' hollowed countenance. He reached for a pill. "If I didn't oblige the peerage," he said thickly, "I'd be begging my bread in Underground and someone would be in this office who'd never tell them no."

Flandry paused. He started a fresh cigarette with unnecessary concentration. *I suppose I am being unjust to him,* he thought. *Poor devil. It can't be much fun being Fenross.*

Still, he reflected, Aycharaych had left the Solar System so smoothly that the space ambush had never even detected his boat. Twenty-odd hours ago, a battered scoutship had limped in to tell the Imperium that Vixen had perforce surrendered to its nameless besiegers, who had landed en masse after reducing the defenses. The last dispatch from Syrax described clashes which had cost the Terrans more ships than the Merseians. Jupiter blazed a mystery in the evening sky. Rumor said that after his human guests had left, Ruethen and his staff had rolled out huge barrels of bitter ale and caroused like trolls for many hours; they must have known some reason to be merry.

You couldn't blame Fenross much. But would the whole long climb of man, from jungle to stars, fall back in destruction—and no single person even deserve to have his knuckles rapped for it?

"What about the reinforcements that were being sent to Vixen?" asked Flandry.

"They're still on their way." Fenross gulped his pill and relaxed a trifle. "What information we have, about enemy strength and so on, suggests that another standoff will develop. The aliens won't be strong enough to kick our force out of the system—"

"Not with Tom Walton in command. I hear he is." A very small warmth trickled into Flandry's soul.

"Yes. At the same time, now the enemy is established on Vixen, there's no obvious way to get them off without total blasting—which would sterilize the planet. Of course, Walton can try to cut their supply lines and starve them out; but once they get their occupation organized, Vixen itself will supply them. Or he can try to find out where they come from, and counter-attack their home. Or perhaps he can negotiate something. I don't know. The Emperor himself gave Admiral Walton what amouts to *carte blanche*."

*It must have been one of His Majesty's off days*, decided Flandry. *Actually doing the sensible thing.*

"Our great handicap is that our opponents know all about us and we know almost nothing about them," went on

Fenross. "I'm afraid the primary effort of our Intelligence must be diverted toward Jupiter for the time being. But someone has to gather information at Vixen too, about the aliens." His voice jerked to a halt.

Flandry filled his lungs with smoke, held it a moment, and let it out in a slow flood. "Eek," he said tonelessly.

"Yes. That's your next assignment."

"But . . . me, alone, to Vixen? Surely Walton's force carries a bunch of our people."

"Of course. They'll do what they can. But parallel operations are standard espionage procedure, as even you must know. Furthermore, the Vixenites made the dramatic rather than the logical gesture. After their planet had capitulated, they got one boat out, with one person aboard. The boat didn't try to reach any Terrestrial ship within the system. That was wise, because the tiny force Aldebaran had sent was already broken in battle and reduced to sneak raids. But neither did the Vixenite boat go to Aldebaran itself. No, it came straight here, and the pilot expected a personal audience with the Emperor."

"And didn't get it," foretold Flandry. "His Majesty is much too busy gardening to waste time on a mere commoner representing a mere planet. "

"Gardening?" Fenross blinked.

"I'm told His Majesty cultivates beautiful pansies," murmured Flandry.

Fenross gulped and said in great haste, "Well, no, of course not. I mean, I myself interviewed the pilot, and read the report carried along. Not too much information, though helpful. However, while Walton has a few Vixenite refugees along as guides and advisors, this pilot is the only one who's seen the aliens close up, on the ground, digging in and trading rifle shots with humans; has experienced several days of occupation before getting away. Copies of the report can be sent after Walton. But that firsthand knowledge of enemy behavior, regulations, all the little unpredictable details . . . that may also prove essential."

"Yes," said Flandry. "If a spy is to be smuggled back

into Vixen's surface. Namely me."

Fenross allowed himself a prim little smile. "That's what I had in mind."

Flandry nodded, unsurprised. Fenross would never give up trying to get him killed. Though in all truth, Dominic Flandry doubtless had more chance of pulling such a stunt and getting back unpunctured than anyone else.

He said idly, "The decision to head straight for Sol wasn't illogical. If the pilot had gone to Aldebaran, then Aldebaran would have sent us a courier reporting the matter and asking for orders. A roundabout route. This way, we got the news days quicker. No, that Vixenite has a level head on his shoulders."

"Hers," corrected Fenross.

"Huh?" Flandry sat bolt upright.

"She'll explain any details," said Fenross. "I'll arrange an open requisition for you; draw what equipment you think you'll need. And if you survive, remember, I'll want every millo's worth accounted for. Now get out and get busy! I've got work to do."

## CHAPTER VII

THE *Hooligan* snaked out of Terran sky, ran for a time on primary drive at an acceleration which it strained the internal grav-field to compensate for, and, having reached a safe distance from Sol, sprang over into secondary. Briefly the viewscreens went wild with Doppler effect and aberration. Then their circuits adapted to the rate at which the vessel pulsed in and out of normal space-time-energy levels; they annulled the optics of pseudo-speed, and Flandry looked again upon cold many-starred night as if he were at rest.

He left Chives in the turret to make final course adjustments, and strolled down to the saloon. "All clear," he smiled. "Estimated time to Vixen, thirteen standard days."

"What?" The girl, Catherine Kittredge, half rose from the luxuriously cushioned bench. "But it took me a month the other way, an' I had the fastest racer on our planet."

"I've tinkered with this one," said Flandry. "Or, rather, found experts to do so." He sat down near her, crossing long legs and leaning an elbow on the mahogany table which the bench half-circled. "Give me a screwdriver and I'll make any firearm in the cosmos sit up and speak. But space drives have an anatomy I can only call whimsical."

He was trying to put her at ease. Poor kid, she had seen her home assailed, halfway in from the Imperial marches that were supposed to bear all the wars; she had seen friends and kinfolk slain in battle with unhuman unknowns, and heard the boots of an occupying enemy racket in once-familiar streets; she had fled to Terra like a child to its mother, and been coldly interviewed in an office and straightway bundled onto a spaceship, with one tailed alien and one suave stranger. Doubtless an official had told her she was a brave little girl and now it was her duty to return as a spy and quite likely be killed. And meanwhile rhododendrons bloomed like cool fire in Terra's parks, and the laughing youth of Terra's aristocracy flew past on their way to some newly opened pleasure house.

No wonder Catherine Kittredge's eyes were wide and bewildered.

They were her best feature, Flandry decided; large, set far apart, a gold-flecked hazel under long lashes and thick dark brows. Her hair would have been nice too, a blonde helmet, if she had not cut it off just below the ears. Otherwise she was nothing much to look at—a broad, snub-nosed, faintly freckled countenance, generous mouth and good chin. As nearly as one could tell through a shapeless gray coverall, she was of medium height and on the stocky side. She spoke

Anglic with a soft regional accent that sounded good in her low voice; but all her mannerisms were provincial, fifty years out of date. Flandry wondered a little desperately what they could talk about.

Well, there was business enough. He flicked buttons for autoservice. "What are you drinking?" he asked. "We've anything within reason, and a few things out of reason, on board."

She blushed. "Nothin', thank you," she mumbled.

"Nothing at all? Come, now. Daiquiri? Wine? Beer? Buttermilk, for heaven's sake?"

"Hm?" She raised a fleeting glance. He discovered Vixen had no dairy industry, cattle couldn't survive there, and dialed ice cream for her. He himself slugged down a large gin-and-bitters. He was going to need alcohol—two weeks alone in space with Little Miss Orphan!

She was pleased enough by discovering ice cream to relax a trifle. Flandry offered a cigarette, was refused, and started one for himself. "You'll have plenty of time to brief me en route," he said, "so don't feel obliged to answer questions now, if it distresses you."

Catherine Kittredge looked beyond him, out the viewscreen and into the frosty sprawl of Andromeda. Her lips twitched downward ever so faintly. But she replied with a steadiness he liked, "Why not? 'Twon't bother me more'n sittin' an' broodin'."

"Good girl. Tell me, how did you happen to carry the message?"

"My brother was our official courier. You know how 'tis on planets like ours, without much population or money; whoever's got the best spaceship gets a subsidy an' carries any special dispatches. I helped him. We used to go off jauntin' for days at a time, an'—No," she broke off. Her fists closed. "I *won't* bawl. The aliens forced a landin'. Hank went off with our groun' forces. He didn't come back. Sev'ral days after the surrender, when things began to settle down a little, I got the news he'd been killed in action. A few of us decided the Imperium had better be given what information we could supply. Since I knew Hank's ship best, they tol' me to go."

"I see." Flandry determined to keep this as dry as possible, for her sake. "I've a copy of the report your people made up, of course, but you had all the way to Sol to study it, so you must know more about it than anyone else off Vixen. Just to give me a rough preliminary idea, I understand some of the invaders knew Anglic and there was a certain amount of long-range parleying. What did they call themselves?"

"Does that matter?" she asked listlessly.

"Not in the faintest, at the present stage of things, except that it's such a weary cliché to speak of Planet X."

She smiled, a tiny bit. "They called themselves the Ardazirho, an' we gathered the *ho* was a collective endin'. So we figure their planet is named Ardazir. Though I can't come near pronouncin' it right."

Flandry took a stereopic from the pocket of his iridescent shirt. It had been snapped from hiding, during the ground battle. Against a background of ruined human homes crouched a single enemy soldier. Warrior? Acolyte? Unit? Armed, at least, and a killer of men.

Preconceptions always got in the way. Flandry's first startled thought had been *Wolf!* Now he realized that of course the Ardazirho was not lupine, didn't even look notably wolfish. Yet the impression lingered. He was not surprised when Catherine Kittredge said the aliens had gone howling into battle.

The were described as man-size bipeds, but digitigrade, which gave their feet almost the appearance of a dog's walking on its hind legs. The shoulders and arms were very humanoid, except that the thumbs were on the opposite side of the hands from mankind's. The head, arrogantly held on a powerful neck, was long and narrow for an intelligent animal, with a low forehead, most of the brain space behind the pointed ears. A black-nosed muzzle, not as sharp as a wolf's and yet somehow like it, jutted out of the face. Its lips were pulled back in a snarl, showing bluntly pointed fangs which suggested a flesh-eater turned omnivore. The eyes were oval, close set, and gray as sleet. Short thick fur covered the entire body, turning to a ruff at the throat; it was rusty red.

"Is this a uniform?" asked Flandry.

The girl leaned close to see. The pictured Ardazirho wore a sort of kilt in checkerboard squares of various hues. Flandry winced at some of the combinations: rose next to scarlet, a glaring crimson offensively between two delicate yellows. "Barbarians indeed," he muttered. "I hope Chives can stand the shock." Otherwise the being was dressed in boots of flexible leather and a harness from which hung various pouches and equipment. He was armed with what was obviously a magnetronic rifle, and had a wicked-looking knife at his belt.

"I'm not sure," said the girl. "Either they don't use uniforms at all, or they have such a variety that we've not made any sense of it. Some might be dressed more or less like him, others in a kind o' tunic an' burnoose, others in breastplates an' fancy plumed helmets."

"Him," pounced Flandry. "They're all male, then?"

"Yes, sir, seems that way. The groun' fightin' lasted long enough for our biologists to dissect an' analyze a few o' their dead. Accordin' to the report, they're placental mammals. It's clear they're from a more or less terrestroid planet, probably with a somewhat stronger gravity. The eye structure suggests their sun is bright, type A5 or thereabouts. That means they should feel pretty much at home in our badlands." Catherine Kittredge shrugged sadly. "Figure that's why they picked us to start on."

"They might have been conquering for some time," said Flandry. "A hot star like an A5 is no use to humans; and I imagine the F-type like yours is about as cool as they care for. They may well have built up a little coterminous kingdom, a number of B, A, and F suns out in your quadrant, where we don't even have a complete astronomical mapping—let alone having explored much. . . . Hm. Didn't you get a chance to interrogate any live prisoners?"

"Yes. 'Twasn't much use. Durin' the fightin', one of our

regiments did encircle a unit o' theirs an' knock it out with stun beams. When two o' them woke up an' saw they were captured, they died."

"Preconditioning," nodded Flandry. "Go on."

"The rest didn't speak any Anglic, 'cept one who'd picked up a little bit. They questioned him." The girl winced. "I don't figure 'twas very nice. The report says toward the end his heart kept stoppin' an' they'd revive it, but at last he died for good. . . . Anyway, it seems a fair bet he was tellin' the truth. An' he didn't know where his home star was. He could understan' our co-ordinate system, an' translate it into the one they used. But that was zeroed arbitrarily on S Doradus, an' he didn't have any idea about the co-ordinates of Ardazir."

"Memory blank." Flandry scowled. "Probably given to all the enlisted ranks. Such officers as must retain information are conditioned to die on capture. What a merry monarch they've got." He twisted his mustache between nervous fingers. "You know, though, this suggests their home is vulnerable. Maybe we should concentrate on discovering where it is."

The girl dropped her eyes. She lost a little color. "Do you think we can, my lord?" she whispered. "Or are we just goin' to die, too?"

"If the mission involves procedures illegal or immoral, I should have no trouble." Flandry grinned at her. "You can do whatever honorable work is necessary. Between us, why, God help Ardazir. Incidentally, I don't rate a title."

"But they called you Sir Dominic."

"A knighthood is not a patent of nobility. I'm afraid my relationship to the peerage involves a bar sinister. You see, one day my father wandered into this sinister bar, and—" Flandry rambled on, skirting the risqué, until he heard her laugh. Then he laughed back and said, "Good girl! What do they call you at home? Kit, I'll swear. Very well, we're off to the wars, you the Kit and I the caboodle. Now let's scream for Chives to lay out caviar and cheeses. Afterward I'll show you to your stateroom." Her face turned hot, and he added, "Its door locks on the inside."

"Thank you," she said, so low he could scarcely hear it. Smoky lashes fluttered on her cheeks. "When I was told to come—with you—I mean, I didn't know—"

"My dear girl," said Flandry, "credit me with enough experience to identify a holstered needle gun among more attractive curves beneath that coverall."

## CHAPTER VIII

THERE was always something unreal about a long trip through space. Here, for a time, you were alone in the universe. No radio could outpace you and be received, even if unimaginable distance would not soon have drowned it in silence. No other signal existed, except another spaceship, and how would it find you unless your feeble drive-pulsations were by the merest chance detected? A whole fleet might travel many parsecs before some naval base sensed its wake with instruments; your one mote of a craft could hurtle to the ends of creation and never be heard. There was nothing to be seen, no landscape, no weather, simply the enormous endless pageantry of changing constellations, now and then a cold nebular gleam between flashing suns, the curdled silver of the Milky Way and the clotted stars near Sagittarius. Yet you in your shell were warm, dry, breathing sweet recycled air; on a luxury vessel like the *Hooligan*, you might listen to recorded Lysarcian bells, sip Namorian maoth and taste Terran grapes.

Flandry worked himself even less mercifully than he did Chives and Kit. It was the hard, dull grind which must underlie all their hopes; study, rehearsal, analysis of data,

planning and discarding and planning again, until brains
could do no more and thinking creaked to a halt. But then
recreation became pure necessity—and they were two humans
with one unobtrusive servant, cruising among the stars.

Flandry discovered that Kit could give him a workout,
when they played handball down in the hold. And her
stubborn chess game defeated his swashbuckling tactics most
of the time. She had a puckish humor when she wasn't
remembering her planet. Flandry would not soon forget her
thumbnail impression of Vice Admiral Fenross, "A mind
like a mousetrap, only he ought to let some o' those poor
little mice go." She could play the lorr, her fingers dancing
over its twelve primary strings with that touch which brings
out the full ringing resonance of the secondaries; she seemed
to know all the ballads from the old brave days when men
were first hewing their homes out of Vixen's wilderness, and
they were good to hear.

Flandry grew slowly aware that she was not at all bad
looking. She just hadn't been sculped into the monotonously
aristocratic appearance of Terra's high-born ladies. The face,
half boyish, was her own, the body full and supple where it
counted. He swore dismally to himself and went on a more
rigorous calisthenic program.

Slowly the stars formed new patterns. There came a time
when Aldebaran stood like red flame, the brightest object in
all heaven. And then the needle-point of Vixen's sun, the
star named Cerulia, glistened keen and blue ahead. And
Flandry turned from the viewscreen and said quietly, "Two
more days to go. I think we'll have captain's dinner tonight."

"Very good, sir," said Chives. "I took it upon myself to
bring along some live Maine lobster. And I trust the Lieb-
fraumilch '51 will be satisfactory?"

"That's the advantage of having a Shalmuan for your
batman," remarked Flandry to Kit. "Their race has more
sensitive palates than ours. They can't go wrong on vintages."

She smiled, but her eyes were troubled.

Flandry retired to his own cabin and an argument. He
wanted to wear a peach-colored tunic with his white slacks;

Chives insisted that the dark blue, with a gold sash, was more suitable. Chives won, naturally. The man wandered into the saloon, which was already laid out for a feast, and poured himself an apéritif. Music sighed from the recorder, and it was sweet to hear.

A footfall came lightly behind him. He turned and nearly dropped his glass. Kit was entering in a sheer black dinner gown; one veil the color of fire flickered from her waistline. A filigree tiara crowned shining hair, and a bracelet of Old Martian silver coiled massive on her wrist.

"Great hopping electrons," gasped Flandry. "Don't *do* such things without warning! Where did the paintbrush come from to lay on the glamor that thick?"

Kit chuckled and pirouetted. "Chives," she said. "Who else? He's a darlin'. He brought the jew'lry along, an' he's been makin' the dress at odd moments this whole trip."

Flandry shook his head and clicked his tongue. "If Chives would accept manumission, he could set himself up in business, equipping lady spies to seduce poor officers like me. He'd own the galaxy in ten years."

Kit blushed and said hastily, "Did he select the tape too? I always have loved Mendelssohn's Violin Concerto."

"Oh, is that what it is? Nice music for a sentimental occasion, anyway. My department is more the administration of drinks. I prescribe this before dinner: Ansan aurea. Essentially, it's a light dry vermouth, but for once a non-Terran soil has improved the flavor of a Terran plant."

She hesitated. "I don't—I never—"

"Well, high time you began." He did not glance at the viewscreen, where Cerulia shone like steel, but they both knew there might not be many hours left for them to savor existence. She took the glass, sipped, and sighed.

"Thank you, Dominic. I've been missin' out on such a lot."

They seated themselves. "We'll have to make that up, after this affair is over," said Flandry. A darkening passed through him, just long enough to make him add, "However, I suspect that on the whole you've done better in life than I."

"What do you mean?" Her eyes above the glass, reflected

the wine's hue and became almost golden.

"Oh . . . hard to say." His mouth twisted ruefully upward. "I've no romantic illusions about the frontier. I've seen too much of it. I'd a good deal rather loll in bed sipping my morning chocolate than bounce into the fields before dawn to cultivate the grotch or scag the thimbs or whatever dreary technicalities it is that pioneers undergo. And yet, well, I've no illusions about my own class either, or my own way of life. You frontier people are the healthy ones. You'll be around—most of you—long after the Empire is a fireside legend. I envy you that."

He broke off. "Pardon me. I'm afraid spiritual jaundice is an occupational disease in my job."

"Which I'm still not sure what is—Oh, dear." Kit chuckled. "Does alcohol act that fast? But really, Dominic, I wish you'd talk a little about your work. All you've said is, you're in Naval Intelligence. I'd like to know what you do."

"Why?" he asked.

She flushed and blurted, "To know you better."

Flandry saw her confusion and moved to hide it from them both, "There's not a lot to tell. I'm a field agent, which means I go out and peek through windows instead of sitting in an office reading the reports of window peekers. Thanks to the circumstance that my immediate superior doesn't like me, I spend most of my working time away from Terra, on what amounts to a roving commission. Good old Fenross. If he was ever replaced by some kindly father-type who dealt justly with all subordinates, I'd dry up and blow away."

"I think that's revoltin'." Anger flashed in her voice.

"What? The discrimination? But my dear lass, what is any civilization but an elaborate structure of special privileges? I've learned to make my way around among them. Good frogs, d'you think I *want* a nice secure desk job with a guaranteed pension?"

"But still, Dominic—a man like you, riskin' his life again an' again, sent almost alone against all Ardazir . . . because someone doesn't like you!" Her face still burned, and there was a glimmer of tears in the hazel eyes.

"Hard to imagine how that could be," said Flandry with calculated smugness. He added, lightly and almost automatically, "But after all, think what an outrageous special privilege your personal heredity represents, so much beauty, charm, and intelligence lavished on one little girl."

She grew mute, but faintly she trembled. With a convulsive gesture, she tossed off her glass.

*Easy, boy,* thought Flandry. A not unpleasurable alertness came to life. *Emotional scenes are the last thing we want out here.* "Which brings up the general topic of you," he said in his chattiest tone. "A subject well worth discussing over the egg flower soup which I see Chives bringing in . . . or any other course, for that matter. Let's see, you were a weather engineer's assistant for a living, isn't that right? Sounds like fun, in an earnest high-booted way." *And might prove useful,* added that part of him which never took a vacation.

She nodded, as anxious as he to escape what they had skirted. They took pleasure in the meal, and talked of many things. Flandry confirmed his impression that Kit was not an unsophisticated peasant. She didn't know the latest delicious gossip about you-know-who and that actor. But she had measured the season of her strange violent planet; she could assemble a machine so men could trust their lives to it; she had hunted and sported, seen birth and death; the intrigues of her small city were as subtle as any around the Imperial throne. Withal, she had the innocence of most frontier folk— or call it optimism, or honor, or courage—at any rate, she had not begun to despair of the human race.

But because he found himself in good company, and this was a special occasion, he kept both their glasses filled. After a while he lost track of how many times he had poured.

When Chives cleared the table and set out coffee and liqueur, Kit reached eagerly for her cup. "I need this," she said, not quite clearly. " 'Fraid I had too much to drink."

"That was the general idea," said Flandry. He accepted a cigar from Chives. The Shalmuan went noiselessly out. Flandry looked across the table. Kit sat with her back to the broad viewscreen, so that the stars were like jewels clustered around her tiara.

"I don't believe it," she said after a moment.

"You're probably right," said Flandry. "What don't you believe?"

"What you were sayin' . . . 'bout the Empire bein' doomed."

"It's better not to believe that," he said gently.

"Not because o' Terra," she said. She leaned forward. The light was soft on her bare young shoulders. "The little bit I saw there was a hard blow. But Dominic, as long's the Empire has men like, like you—we'll take on the whole universe an' win."

"Blessings," said Flandry in haste.

"No." Her eyes were the least bit hazed, but they locked steadily with his. She smiled, more in tenderness than mirth. "You won't wriggle off the hook with a joke this time, Dominic. You gave me too much to drink, you see, an'—I mean it. A planet with you on its side has still got hope enough."

Flandry sipped his liqueur. Suddenly the alcohol touched his own brain with its pale fires, and he thought, *Why not be honest with her? She can take it. Maybe she even deserves it.*

"No, Kit," he said. "I know my class from the inside out, because it is my class and I probably wouldn't choose another even if some miracle made me able to. But we're hollow, and corrupt, and death has marked us for its own. Ultimately, though we disguise it, however strenuous and hazardous and even lofty our amusements are, the only reason we can find for living is to have fun. And I'm afraid that isn't reason enough."

"But it is!" she cried.

"You think so," he said, "because you're lucky enough to belong to a society which still has important jobs uncompleted. But we aristocrats of Terra, we enjoy life instead of enjoying what we're doing . . . and there's a cosmos of difference.

"The measure of our damnation is that every one of us with an intelligence—and there are some—every one sees the Long Night coming. We've grown too wise; we've studied a little psychodynamics, or perhaps only read a lot of history, and we can see that Manuel's Empire was not a glorious resurgence. It was the Indian summer of Terran civilization. (But you've never seen Indian summer, I suppose. A pity; no planet has anything more beautiful and full of old magics.) Now even that short season is past. Autumn is far along; the nights are cold and the leaves are fallen and the last escaping birds call through a sky which has lost all color. And yet, we who see winter coming can also see it won't be here till after our lifetimes . . . so we shiver a bit, and swear a bit, and go back to playing with a few bright dead leaves."

He stopped. Silence grew around them. And then, from the intercom, music began again, a low orchestral piece which spoke to deep places of their awareness.

"Excuse me," said Flandry. "I really shouldn't have wished my sour pessimism on you."

Her smile this time held a ghost of pity. "An' o' course 'twouldn't be debonair to show your real feelin's, or try to find words for them."

"*Touché!*" He cocked his head. "Think we could dance to that?"

"The music? Hardly. The *Liebestod* is background for somethin' else. I wonder if Chives knew."

"Hm?" Flandry looked surprised at the girl.

"I don't mind at all," she whispered. "Chives is a darlin'."

Suddenly he understood.

But the stars were chill behind her. Flandry thought of guns and dark fortresses waiting for them both. He thought of knightly honor, which would not take advantage of the helplessness which is youth—and then, with a little sadness, he decided that practical considerations were what really turned the balance for him.

He raised the cigar to his mouth and said softly, "Better drink your coffee before it gets cold, lass."

With that, the moment was safely over. He thought he saw disappointed gratitude in Kit's hurried glance, but wasn't sure. She turned around, gazing at the stars merely to avoid facing him for the next few seconds.

Her breath sighed outward. She sat looking at Cerulia for

a whole minute. Then she stared down at her hand and said tonelessly, "Figure you're right 'bout the Empire. But then what's to become o' Vixen?"

"We'll liberate it, and squeeze a fat indemnity out of Ardazir," said Flandry as if there were no doubt.

"Uh-uh." She shook her head. Bitterness began to edge her voice. "Not if 'tisn't convenient. Your Navy might decide to fight the war out where 'tis. An' then my whole planet, my people, the little girl next door an' her kitten, trees an' flowers an' birds, why, 'twill just be radioactive ash blowin' over dead gary hills. Or maybe the Imperium will decide to compromise, an' let Ardazir keep Vixen. Why not? What's one planet to the Empire? A swap might, as you say, buy them peace in their own lifetimes. A few million human bein's, that's nothin', write them off in red ink." She shook her head again in a dazed way. "Why are we goin' there, you an' I? What are we workin' for? Whatever we do can come to nothin', from one stroke of a pen in some bored bureaucrat's hand. Can't it?"

"Yes," said Flandry.

## CHAPTER IX

CERULIA, being a main-sequence star, did not need vastly more mass than Sol to shine more fiercely. Vixen, the fourth planet out, circled its primary in one and a half standard years, along such an orbit that it received, on the average, about as much radiation as Terra.

"The catch lies in that word 'average,' " murmured Flandry.

He floated in the turret with Chives, hands on the control panel and body weightless in a cocoon of pilot harness. To port, the viewscreens were dimmed, lest the harsh blue sun burn out his eyes. Elsewhere, distorted constellations sprawled stark against night. Flandry picked out the Jupiter-type planet called Ogre by the humans of Vixen: a bright yellow glow, its larger moons visible like sparks. And what were its Ymirite colonists thinking?

"Ogre's made enough trouble for Vixen all by itself," complained Flandry. "Its settlers ought to be content with that, and not go plotting with Ardazir. If they are, I mean." He turned to Chives. "How's Kit taking this free-fall plunge?"

"I regret to say Miss Kittredge did not look very comfortable, sir," answered the Shalmuan. "But she said she was."

Flandry clicked his tongue. Since the advent of gravity control, there had been little need for civilians ever to undergo weightlessness; hence Kit, susceptible to it didn't have the training that would have helped. Well, she'd be a lot sicker if an Ardazirho missile homed on the *Hooligan*. Nobody ever died of space nausea: no such luck!

Ardazir would undoubtedly have mounted tight guard over conquered Vixen. Flandry's detectors were confirming this. The space around the planet quivered with primary-drive vibrations, patrolling warcraft, and there must be a network of orbital robot monitors to boot. A standard approach was certain to be spotted. There was another way to land, though, if you were enough of a pilot and had enough luck. Flandry had decided to go ahead with it, rather than contact Walton's task force. He couldn't do much there except report himself in . . . and then proceed to Vixen anyway, with still more likelihood of detection and destruction.

Engines cold, the *Hooligan* plunged at top meteoric velocity straight toward her goal. Any automaton was sure to register her as a siderite, and ignore her. Only visual observation would strip that disguise off; and space is so vast that even with the closest blockade, there was hardly a chance of passing that close to an unwarned enemy. Escape from the surface would be harder, but this present stunt was foolproof. Until you hit atmosphere!

Flandry watched Vixen swelling in the forward viewscreens. To one side Cerulia burned, ominously big. The planet's northern day-side was like a slice of incandescence; polarizing telescopes showed bare mountains, stony deserts, rivers gone wild with melted snows. In the southern hemisphere, the continents were still green and brown, the oceans deeply blue, like polished cobalt. But cloud banded that half of the world, storms marched roaring over hundreds of kilometers, lightning flared through rain. The equator was hidden under a nearly solid belt of cloud and gale. The northern aurora was cold flame; the south pole, less brilliant, still shook great banners of light into heaven. A single small moon, 100,000 kilometers from the surface, looked pale against that luminance.

The spaceship seemed tomb silent when Flandry switched his attention back to it. He said, just to make a noise, "And this passes for a terrestroid, humanly habitable planet. What real estate agents they must have had in the pioneer days!"

"I understand that southern Cerulia IV is not unsalubrious most of the year, sir," said Chives. "It is only now, in fact, that the northern part becomes lethal."

Flandry nodded. Vixen was the goat of circumstance; huge Ogre had exactly four times the period, and thus over millions of years resonance had multiplied perturbation and brought the eccentricity of Vixen's orbit close to one-half. The planet's axial inclination was 24°, and northern midsummer fell nearly at periastron. Thus, every eighteen months, Cerulia scorched that hemisphere with fourfold the radiation Terra got from Sol. This section of the orbit was hastily completed, and most of Vixen's year was spent in cooler regions. "But I dare say the Ardazirho timed their invasion for right now," said Flandry. "If they're from an A-type star, the northern weather shouldn't be too hard on them."

He put out his final cigarette. The planet filled the bow screen. Robot mechanisms could do a lot, but now there must also be live piloting . . . or a streak in Vixen's sky and a crater blasted from its rock.

At the *Hooligan's* speed, she crossed the tenuous upper air layers and hit stratosphere in a matter of seconds. It was like a giant's fist. Flandry's harness groaned as his body hurtled forward. There was no outside noise, yet, but the flitter herself shrieked in metallic pain. The screens became one lurid fire, air heated to incandescence.

Flandry's arm trembled with weight. He slammed it down on the drive switches. Chives' slight form could not stir under these pressures, but the green tail darted, button to dial to vernier. Engines bellowed as they fought to shed velocity. The vessel glowed red; but her metal was crystallized to endure more than furnace heat. Thunder banged around her, within her. Flandry felt his ribs shoved toward his lungs, as direction shifted. Still he could see only flame outside. But his blurring eyes read instruments. He knew the vessel had leveled off, struck denser atmosphere, skipped like a stone, and was now rounding the planet in monstrous shuddering bounces.

Only then did he have time to reactivate the internal compensators. A steady one gee poured its benediction through him. He drew unsteady breath into an aching chest. "For this we get *paid?*" he mumbled.

While Chives took over, and the thermostat brought the turret near an endurable temperature, Flandry unbuckled and went below to Kit's stateroom. She lay unstirring in harness, a trickle of blood from the snub nose. He injected her with stimulol. Her eyes fluttered open. She looked so young and helpless that he had to glance away. "Sorry to jolt you back to consciousness in this fashion," he said. "It's bad practice. But right now, we need a guide."

"O' course." She preceded him to the turret. He sat down and she leaned over his shoulder, frowning at the viewscreens. The *Hooligan* burrowed into atmosphere on a steep downward slant. The roar of cloven air boomed through the hull. Mountains rose jagged on a night horizon. "That's the Ridge," said Kit. "Head yonder, over Moonstone Pass." On the other side, a shadowed valley gleamed with rivers, under stars and a trace of aurora. "There's the Shaw, an' the King's Way cuttin' through. Land anywhere near, 'tisn't likely the boat will be found."

The Shaw belied its name; it was a virgin forest, 40,000 square kilometers of tall trees. Flandry set his craft down so gently that not a twig was broken, cut the engines and leaned back. "Thus far," he breathed gustily, "we is did it, chillun!"

"Sir," said Chives, "may I once again take the liberty of suggesting that if you and the young lady go off alone, without me, you need a psychiatrist."

"And may I once again tell you where to stick your head," answered Flandry. "I'll have trouble enough passing myself off as a Vixenite, without you along. You stay with the boat and keep ready to fight. Or, more probably, to scramble out of here like an egg."

He stood up. "We'd better start now, Kit," he added. "That drug won't hold you up for very many hours."

Both humans were already dressed in the soft green coveralls Chives had made according to Kit's description of professional hunters. That would also explain Flandry's little radio transceiver, knife and rifle; his accent might pass for that of a man lately moved here from the Avian Islands. It was a thin enough disguise . . . but the Ardazirho wouldn't have an eye for fine details. The main thing was to reach Kit's home city, Garth, undetected. Once based there, Flandry could assess the situation and start making trouble.

Chives wrung his hands, but bowed his master obediently out the airlock. It was midwinter, but also periastron; only long nights and frequent rains marked the season in this hemisphere. The forest floor was thick and soft underfoot. Scant light came through the leaves, but here and there on the high trunks glowed yellow phosphorescent fungi, enough to see by. The air was warm, full of strange green scents. Out in the darkness there went soft whistlings, callings, croakings, patterings, once a scream which cut off in a gurgle, the sounds of a foreign wilderness.

It was two hours' hike to the King's Way. Flandry and Kit fell into the rhythm of it and spoke little. But when they finally came out on the broad starlit ribbon of road, her hand stole into his. "Shall we walk on?" She asked.

"Not if Garth is fifty kilometers to go," said Flandry. He sat down by the road's edge. She lowered herself into the curve of his arm.

"Are you cold?" he asked, feeling her shiver.

" 'Fraid," she admitted.

His lips brushed hers. She responded shyly, unpracticed. It beat hiking. Or did it? *I never liked hors d'oeuvres alone for a meal,* thought Flandry, and drew her close.

Light gleamed far down the highway. A faint growl waxed. Kit disengaged herself. "Saved by the bell," murmured Flandry, "but don't stop to wonder which of us was." She laughed, a small and trembling sound beneath unearthly constellations.

Flandry got up and extended his arm. The vehicle ground to a halt and the driver of the ten-cartruck leaned out. "Boun' for Garth?" he called.

"That's right." Flandry helped Kit into the cab and followed. The truck started again, its train rumbling for 200 meters behind.

"Goin' to turn in your gun, are you?" asked the driver. He was a burly bitter-faced man. One arm carried the traces of a recent blaster wound.

"Figure so," Kit replied. "My husban' an' I been trekkin' in the Ridge this last three months. We heard 'bout the invasion an' started back, but floods held us up—rains, you know— an' our radio's given some trouble too. So we aren't sure o' what's been happenin'."

"Enough." The driver spat out the window. He glanced sharply at them. "But what the gamma would anybody be doin' in the mountains this time o' year?"

Kit began to stammer. Flandry said smoothly, "Keep it confidential, please, but this is when the cone-tailed radcat comes off the harl. It's dangerous, yes, but we've filled six caches of grummage."

"Hm . . . uh . . . yeh. Sure. Well, when you reach Garth, better not carry your gun yourself to the wolf headquarters.

They'll most likely shoot you first an' ask your intentions later. Lay it down somewhere an' go ask one o' them would he please be so kind as to come take it away from you."

"I hate to give up this rifle," said Flandry.

The driver shrugged. "Keep it, then, if you want to take the risk. But not aroun' me. I fought at Burnt Hill, an' played dead all night while those howlin' devils hunted the remnants of our troop. Then I got home somehow, an' that's enough. I got a wife an' children to keep." He jerked his thumb backward. "Load o' rare earth ore this trip. The wolves'll take it, an' Hobden's mill will turn it into fire-control elements for 'em, an' they'll shoot some more at the Empire's ships. Sure, call me a quislin'—an' then wait till you've seen your friends run screamin' down your street with a pack o' batsnakes flappin' an' snappin' at them an' the wolves boundin' behind laughin'. Ask yourself if you want to go through that, for an Empire that's given us up already."

"Has it?" asked Flandry. "I understood from one 'cast that there were reinforcements coming."

"Sure. They're here. One o' my chums has a pretty good radio, an' sort o' followed the space battle when Walton's force arrived, by receivin' stray messages. It petered out pretty quick, though. What can Walton do, unless he attacks this planet, where the wolves are now based, where they're already makin' their own supplies an' munitions? An' if he does that—" The headlight reflections shimmered off sweat on the man's face. "No more Vixen. Just a cinder. You pray God, chum, that the Terrans don't try to blast Ardazir off Vixen."

"What's happening, then, in space?" asked Flandry.

He didn't expect a coherent reply. To the civilian, as to the average fighter, war is one huge murky chaos. It was a pure gift when the driver said, "My chum caught radio 'casts beamed at us from the Terran fleet. The wolves tried to jam it, o' course, but I heard an' figure 'tis mostly truth. Because 'tis bad enough! There was a lot o' guff about keepin' up our courage, an' sabotagin' the enemy, an'—" The driver rasped an obscenity. "Sorry, ma'm. But wait till you see what 'tis really like arou' Garth an' you'll know how I feel about *that* idea. Admiral Walton says his fleet's seized some asteroid bases an' theirs isn't tryin' to get him off 'em. Stalemate, you see, till the wolves have built up enough strength. Which they're doin', fast. The reason the admiral can't throw everything he's got against them in space is that he has to watch Ogre too. Seems there's reason to suspect Ymir might be in cahoots with Ardazir. The Ymirites aren't sayin'. You know what they're like."

Flandry nodded. "Yes. 'If you will not accept our word that we are neutral, there is no obvious way to let you convince yourselves, since the whole Terran Empire could not investigate a fraction of Dispersal territory. Accordingly, we shall not waste our time discussing the question.' "

"That's it, chum. You've got the very tone. They might be honest, sure. Or they might be waitin' for the minute Walton eases up his watch on 'em, to jump him."

Flandry glanced out. The stars flashed impersonally, not caring that a few motes of flesh named them provinces for a few centuries. He saw that part of this planet's sky which had no stars, a hole into forever. Kit had told him it was called the Hatch. But that was only a nearby dark nebula, not even a big one. The clear white spark of Rigel was more sinister, blazing from the heart of Merseia's realm. And what of Ogre, tawny above the trees?

"What do you think will happen?" Kit's voice could scarcely be heard through the engine grumble.

"I don't even dare guess," said the driver. "Maybe Walton'll negotiate something—might leave us here, to become wolf-cattle, or might arrange to evacuate us an' we can become beggars on Terra. Or he might fight in space . . . but even if he doesn't attack their forts here on Vixen, we'll all be hostages to Ardazir, won't we? Or the Ymirites might attack. . . . No, ma'm, I'm just drivin' my truck an' drawin' my pay an' feedin' my family. Shorter rations every week, it seems. Figure there's nothin' else any one person can do. Is there?"

Kit began to cry, a soft hopeless sobbing on Flandry's

shoulder. He laid an arm around her and they sat thus all the way to Garth.

## CHAPTER X

NIGHT again, after a short hot winter day full of thunderstorms. Flandry and Emil Bryce stood in the pit blackness of an alley, watching a nearly invisible street. Rain sluiced over their cloaks. A fold in Flandry's hood was letting trickle in, his tunic was soaked, but he dared not move. At any moment now, the Ardazirho would come by.

The rain roared slow and heavy, down over the high-peaked roofs of Garth, through blacked-out streets and gurgling into the storm drains. All wind had stopped, but now and then lightning glared. There was a brief white view of pavement that shimmered wet, half-timbered houses with blind shutters crowded side by side, a skeletal transmitter tower for one of the robotic weather-monitor stations strewn over the planet. Then night clamped back down, and thunder went banging through enormous hollow spaces.

Emil Bryce had not moved for half an hour. But he really was a hunter by trade, thought Flandry. The Terran felt an unreasonable resentment of Bryce's guild. Damn them, it wasn't fair, in that trade they stood waiting for prey since they were boys—and *he* had to start cold. No, hot. It steamed beneath his rain cape.

Feet resounded on the walk. They did not have a human rhythm. And they did not smack the ground first with a boot heel, but clicked metal-shod toes along the pavement.

A flashbeam bobbed, slashing darkness with a light too blue and sharp for human comfort. Watery reflections touched Bryce's broad red face. His mouth alone moved, and Flandry could read fear upon it. *Wolves!*

But Bryce's dart gun slithered from under his cloak. Flandry eased steel knucks onto one hand. With the other, he gestured Bryce back. He, Flandry, must go first, pick out the precise enemy he wanted—in darkness, in rain, and all their faces nonhuman. Nor would uniforms help; the Ardazirho bore such a wild variety of dress.

But . . . Flandry was trained. It had been worth a rifle, to have an excuse for entering local invader headquarters. Their garrison in Garth was not large: a few hundred, for a city of a quarter million. But modern heavy weapons redressed that, robotanks, repeating cannon, the flat announcement that any town where a human uprising actually succeeded would be missiled. (The glassy crater which had been Marsburg proved it.) The Garth garrison was there chiefly to man observation posts and anti-spacecraft defenses in the vicinity; but they also collected firearms, directed factories to produce for their army, prowled in search of any citizens with spirit left to fight. Therefore, Flandry told himself, their chief officer must have a fair amount of knowledge—and the chief officer spoke Anglic, and Flandry had gotten a good look at him while surrendering the rifle, and Flandry was trained to tell faces apart, even nonhuman faces—

And now Clanmaster Temulak, as he had called himself, was going off duty, from headquarters to barracks. Bryce and others had been watching the Ardazirho for weeks. They had told Flandry that the invaders went on foot, in small armed parties, whenever practicable. Nobody knew quite why. Maybe they preferred the intimacy with odors and sounds which a vehicle denied; it was known they had better noses than man. Or perhaps they relished the challenge; more than once, humans had attacked such a group, been beaten off and hunted down and torn to pieces. Civilians had no chance against body armor, blast-weapons, and reflexes trained for combat.

*But I'm not a civilian,* Flandry told himself, *and Bryce has some rather special skills.*

The quarry passed by. Scattered flashbeam light etched the ruffed, muzzled heads against flowing dimness. There were five. Flandry identified Temulak, helmeted and corseleted, near the middle. He glided out of the alley, behind them.

The Ardazirho whipped about. How keen were their ears? Flandry kept going. One red-furred alien hand dropped toward a holstered blaster. Flandry smashed his steel-knuckled fist at Temulak's face. The enemy bobbed his head, the knucks clanged off the helmet. And light metal sheathed his belly, no blow would have effect there. The blaster came out. Flandry chopped down his left palm, edge on, with savage precision. He thought he felt wristbones crack beneath it. Temulak's gun clattered to the pavement. The Ardazirho threw back his head and howled, ululating noise hurled into the rain. And Headquarters only half a kilometer away, barracks no further in the opposite direction—

Flandry threw a karate kick to the jaw. The officer staggered back. But he was quick, twisting about to seize the man's ankle before it withdrew. They went down together. Temulak's right hand still hung useless, but his left snatched for Flandry's throat. The Terran glimpsed fingernails reinforced with sharp steel plectra. He threw up an arm to keep his larynx from being torn out. Temulak howled again. Flandry chopped at the hairy neck. The Ardazirho ducked and sank teeth into Flandry's wrist. Anguish went like flame along the nerves. But now Temulak was crouched before him. Flandry slammed down a rabbit punch. Temulak slumped. Flandry got on his back and throttled him.

Looking up, gasping, the man saw shadows leap and yell in the glow of the dropped flashlight. There had been no way simply to needle Temulak. He was wanted alive, and Flandry didn't know what anesthetics might be fatal to an Ardazirho. But Bryce had only to kill the guards, as noiselessly as possible. His airgun spat cyanide darts, quick death for any oxygen breather. And his skilled aim sent those darts into exposed flesh, not uselessly breaking on armor. Two shapes sprawled in the street. Another had somehow jumped for Bryce's throat. The hunter brought up one boot. It clanged on a breastplate, but sheer force sent the alien lurching backward. Bryce shot him. By then the last one had freed his blaster. It crashed and blazed through rain. Bryce had already dropped. The ion bolt sizzled where he had been. Bryce, fired, missed, rolled away from another blast, fired again and missed. Now howling could be heard down the street, as a pack of invaders rallied to come and help.

Flandry reached across Temulak's gaunt body, picked up the Clanmaster's gun, and waited. He was nearly blind in this night. The other Ardazirho's blaster flamed once more. Flandry fired where it showed. The alien screamed, once, and thudded to the street. Scorched hair and meat smoked sickly in the wet air.

"Out o' here!" gasped Bryce. He sprang erect. "They're comin'! An' they'll track us by scent—"

"I came prepared for *that*," said Flandry. A brief hard grin peeled his teeth. He let Bryce pick up Temulak while he got a flat plastibottle from his tunic. He turned a pressure nozzle and sprayed a liter of gasoline around the area. "If their noses are any good for several minutes after this, I give up. Let's go."

Bryce led the way, through the alley to the next street, down a block of horribly open paving, then hand-over-hand across a garden wall. No private human vehicles could move after dark without being shot at from the air, but it wasn't far to the underground hideout. In fact, too close, thought Flandry. But then, who on Vixen had any experience with such operations? Kit had looked up those friends in Garth who smuggled her out, and they had led Flandry straight to their bitter little organization. It expedited matters this time, yes, but suppose the Ardazirho had supplied a ringer? Or . . . it was only a matter of time before they started questioning humans in detail, under drugs and duress. Then you needed cells, changing passwords, widely scattered boltholes, or your underground was done for.

Flandry stumbled through drenched flower beds. He helped Bryce carry Temulak down into the hurricane cellar; standard for every house in Garth. A tunnel had been dug from this one; its door, at least, was well concealed. Flandry and Bryce groped for several hundred meters to the other end. They emerged beneath a house whose address they should not have been permitted to know.

Judith Hurst turned about with a small shriek when the cellar door opened. Then dim light picked out Bryce's heavy form, and Temulak still limp in the hunter's arms. Flandry came behind, shedding his cape with a relieved whistle. "Oh," gasped Judith. "You got him!"

Bryce's eyes went around the circle of them. A dozen men stood with taut brown faces in the light of a single small fluoro. Their shadows fell monstrous in the corners and across the window shutters. Knives and forbidden guns gleamed at their belts. Kit was the only person seated, still slumped in the dull sadness of stimulol reaction.

"Damn near didn't," grunted Bryce. "Couldn't have, without the captain here. Sir Dominic, I apologize for some things I'd been thinkin' lately 'bout Terra."

"An' I." Judith Hurst trod forward, taking both the Navy man's hands. She was among the few women in the underground, and Flandry thought it a crime to risk such looks being shot up. She was tall, with long auburn hair and skin like cream; her eyes were sleepy brown in a full, pouting face; her figure strained at shorts and bolero. "I never thought I'd see you again," she said. "But you've come back with the first real success this war's had for us."

"Two swallows do not make a drinking bout," warned Flandry. He gave her his courtliest bow. "Speaking of which, I could use something liquid, and cannot imagine a more ornamental cupbearer. But first, let's deal with friend Temulak. This way, isn't it?"

As he passed Kit, her exhausted eyes turned up to him. Slow tears coursed down her face. "Oh, Dominic, you're alive," she whispered. "That makes everything else seem like nothin'." She rose to wobbly legs. He threw her a preoccupied smile and continued on past, his brain choked with technicalities.

Given a proper biopsych lab, he could have learned how to get truth out of Temulak with drugs and electronics. But now he just didn't have data on the species. He would have to fall back on certain widely applicable, if not universal, rules of psychology.

At his orders, an offside room in the cellar had been provided with a comfortable bed. He stripped Temulak and tied him down, firmly, but using soft bonds which wouldn't chafe. The prisoner began to stir. By this time Flandry was through and Temulak immobile, the gray alien eyes were open and the muzzle wrinkled back over white teeth. A growl rumbled in Temulak's throat.

"Feeling better?" asked the man unctuously.

"Not as well as I shall when we pull you down in the street." The Anglic was thickly accented, but fluent, and it bore a haughtiness like steel.

"I shudder." Flandry kindled a cigarette. "Well, comrade, if you want to answer some questions now, it will save trouble all around. I presume, since you're alive, you've been blanked of your home sun's co-ordinates. But you retain clues." He blew a thoughtful smoke ring. "And, to be sure, there are the things you obviously do know, since your rank requires it. Oh, all sorts of things, dear heart, which my side is just dying to find out." He chuckled. "I don't mean that literally. Any dying will be done by you."

Temulak stiffened. "If you think I would remain alive, at the price of betraying the *orbekk*—"

"Nothing so clear-cut."

The red fur bristled, but Temulak snarled: "Nor will pain in any degree compel me. And I do not believe you understand the phychophysiology of my race well enough to undertake total reconditioning."

"No," admitted Flandry, "not yet. However, I haven't time for reconditioning in any event, and torture is so strenuous . . . besides offering no guarantee that when you talk, you won't fib. No, no, my friend, you'll want to spill to me pretty soon. Whenever you've had enough, just call and I'll come hear you out."

He nodded to Dr. Reineke. The physician wheeled forth the equipment he had abstracted from Garth General Hospital at Flandry's request. A blindfolding hood went over Temulak's eyes, sound-deadening wax filled his ears and plugged his nose, a machine supplied him with intravenous nourishment and another removed body wastes. They left him immobile and, except for the soft constant pressure of bonds and bed, sealed into a darkness like death. No sense impressions could reach him from outside. It was painless, it did no permanent harm, but the mind is not intended for such isolation. When there is nothing by which it may orient itself, it rapidly loses all knowledge of time; an hour seems like a day, and later like a week or a year. Space and material reality vanish. Hallucinations come, and the will begins to crumble. Most particularly is this true when the victim is among enemies, tensed to feel the whip or knife which his own ferocious culture would surely use.

Flandry closed the door. "Keep a guard," he said. "When he begins to holler, let me know." He peeled off his tunic. "From whom can I beg something dry to wear?"

Judith gave his torso a long look. "I thought all Terrans were flabby, Sir Dominic," she purred. "I was wrong about that, too."

His eyes raked her. "And you, my dear, make it abundantly plain that Vixenites are anything but," he leered.

She took his arm. "What do you plan to do next?"

"Scratch around. Observe. Whip this maquisard outfit into something efficient. There are so many stunts to teach you. To name just one, any time you've no other amusement, you can halt work at a war factory for half a day with an anonymous telecall warning that a time bomb's been planted and the staff had better get out. Then there's all the rest of your planet to organize. I don't know how many days I'll have, but there's enough work to fill a year of 'em." Flandry stretched luxuriously. "Right now, though, I want that drink I spoke of."

"Here you are, sir." Bryce held out a flask.

Judith flicked a scowl at him. "Is that white mule all you can offer the captain?" she cried. Her hair glowed along her back as she turned to smile again at Flandry. "I know you'll think I'm terribly forward, but I have two bottles o' real Bourgogne at my house. 'Tis only a few blocks from here, an' I know a safe way to go."

*Oh-ho!* Flandry licked his mental chops. "Delighted," he said.

"I'd invite the rest o' you," said Judith sweetly, "but 'tisn't enough to go aroun', an' Sir Dominic deserves it the most. Nothin's too good for him, that's what I think. Just nothin' at all."

"Agreed," said Flandry. He bowed goodnight and went out with her.

Kit stared after them a moment. As he closed the door, he heard her burst into weeping.

## CHAPTER XI

THREE OF Vixen's 22-hour rotation periods went by, and part of a fourth, before the message came that Temulak had broken. Flandry whistled. "It's about time! If they're all as tough as that—"

Judith clung to him. "Do you have to go right now, darlin'?" she murmured. "You've been away so much . . . out prowlin', spyin', an' the streets still full o' packs huntin' for whoever attacked that squad—I'm terrified for you."

He look was more inviting than anxious. Flandry kissed

her absent-mindedly. "We're patriots and all that sort of rot," he said. "I could not love you so much, dear, et cetera. Now do let go." He was out the door before she could speak further.

The way between her house and the underground's went mostly from garden to garden, but there was a stretch of public thoroughfare. Flandry put hands in pockets and sauntered along under rustling feather palms as if he had neither cares nor haste. The other humans about, afoot or in groundcars, were subdued, the pinch of hunger and shabbiness already upon them. Once a party of Ardazirho whirred past on motor unicycles; their sharp red muzzles clove the air like prows, and they left a wake of frightened silence behind them. The winter sun burned low to northwest, big and dazzling white in a pale sky, among hurried stormclouds.

When Flandry let himself into the cellar, only Emil Bryce and Kit Kittredge were there. The hunter lounged on guard. From the closed door behind him came howling and sobbing. "He babbled he'd talk," said Bryce. "But can you trust what he says?"

"Interrogation is a science too," answered Flandry. "If Temulak is enough like a human to break under isolation, he won't be able to invent consistent lies fast enough when I start throwing questions at him. Did you get that recorder I wanted?"

"Here." Kit picked it up. She looked very small and alone in all the shadows. Sleeplessness had reddened her eyes. She brought the machine to Flandry, who met her several meters from Bryce. She leaned toward him on tiptoe and whispered shakily, "What will you do now?"

Flandry studied her. He had gotten to know her well on the journey here, he thought. But that was under just one set of conditions—and how well does one human ever know another, in spite of all pretentious psychology? Since capturing the Adarzirho, he had only seen her on a single brief visit to this cellar. They had had a few moments alone, but nothing very personal was said. There had been no time for it. He saw how she trembled.

"I'm going to quiz brother Temulak," he told her. "And afterward I could use some dinner and a stiff drink."

"With Judith Hurst?" It startled him, how ferociously she spat it out.

"Depends," he said in a careful tone.

"Dominic—" She hugged herself, forlornly, to stop shivering. Her gaze blurred, seeking his. "Don't. Please don't make me do . . . what I don't want—"

"We'll see." He started toward the door. Kit began to cry, hopelessly this time.

Bryce got up. "Why, what all's the matter?" he asked.

"She's overtired." Flandry opened the door.

"Worse'n that." The hunter looked from him to the girl and back again. Resentment smoldered in his growl: "Maybe it's none o' my business—"

"It isn't." Flandry stepped through, closing the door behind him.

Temulak lay shuddering and gasping. Flandry set up the recorder and unplugged the Ardazirho's ears. "Did you want to speak to me?" he asked mildly.

"Let me go!" shrieked Temulak. "Let me go, I say! *Zamara shammish ni ulan!*" He opened his mouth and howled. It was so much like a beast that a crawling went along Flandry's spine.

"We'll see, after you've co-operated." The man sat down.

"I never thought . . . you gray people . . . gray hearts—" Temulak whimpered. He dribbled between his fangs.

"Goodnight, then," said Flandry. "Sweet dreams."

"No! No, let me see! Let me smell! I will . . . *zamara, zamara*—"

Flandry began to interrogate.

It took time. The basic principle was to keep hitting, snap out a question, yank forth the answer, toss the next question, pounce on the smallest discrepancies, always strike and strike and strike with never a second's pause for the victim to think. Without a partner, Flandry was soon tired. He kept going, on cigarettes and nerves; after the first hour, he lost count of time.

In the end, with a full tape, he relaxed a moment. The air was nearly solid with smoke. Sweat felt sticky under his clothes. He puffed yet another cigarette and noticed impersonally the shakiness of his hand. But Temulak whined and twitched, beaten close to mindlessness by sheer psychic exhaustion.

The picture so far was only a bare outline, thought Flandry in a dull far-off way. How much could be told in one night of an entire world, its greatness and rich variety, its many peoples and all their histories? How much, to this day, do we really know about Terra? But the tape held information worth entire ships.

Somewhere there was a sun, brighter even than Cerulia, and a planet called Ardazir by its principal nation. ("Nation" was the Anglic word; Flandry had an impression that "clan alliance" or "pack aggregate" might more closely translate *orbekh*.) Interplanetary travel had been independently achieved by that country. Then, some fifteen standard years ago, gravitics, super-light pseudo-speeds, the whole apparatus of the modern galaxy, had burst upon Ardazir. The war lords (chiefs, speakers, pack leaders?) of Urdahu, the dominant *orbekh,* had promptly used these to complete the subjugation of their own world. Then they turned outward. Their hunters ravened into a dozen backward systems, looting and enslaving; engineers followed, organizing the conquered planets for further war.

And now the attack on the human empire had begun. The lords of Urdahu assured their followers that Ardazir had allies, mighty denizens of worlds so alien that there could never be any fear of attack . . . though these aliens had long been annoyed by humankind, and found in Ardazir an instrument to destroy and replace the Terran Empire. . . . Temulak had not inquired more deeply, had not thought much about it at all. The Ardazirho seemed, by nature, somewhat more reckless and fatalistic than men, and somewhat less curious. If circumstances had provided a chance for adventure, glory, and wealth, that was enough. Precaution could be left in care of the *orbekh's* wise old females.

Flandry smoked in a thick silence. If Ymir were, indeed, behind Ardazir—it would be natural for Ymir to co-operate temporarily with Merseia, whipsawing Terra between the Syrax and Vixen crises. Maybe Merseia was next on Ymir's list. Thereafter Ardazir would hardly prove troublesome to wreck.

But what grudge could Ymir have against oxygen breathers, or even against Terra alone? There had been some small friction, yes, inevitably—but nothing serious, surely the monsters rubbed each other more raw than—*And yet Horx did his level best to kill me. Why? What could he have been hired with? What material thing from a terrestroid planet would not collapse in his hands on Jupiter? What reason would he have, except orders from his own governor, who was carrying out a policy hatched on Ymir itself—?*

Flandry clenched a fist. There was an answer to that question but not one he dared rely on without further proof. He bent his mind back toward practicalities. Mostly the tape held such details: the number of Ardazirho ships and troops in this system, recognition signals, military dispositions across Vixen, the layout of forts and especially of the great head-quarters den; the total population of Ardazir, resources, industry, army and navy—Temulak was not in on many state secrets, but he had enough indications to give Flandry gooseflesh. Two million or so warriors occupied Vixen; a hundred million were still at home or on the already conquered planets, where war material was being rapidly stockpiled; officers had all been informed that there were plenty of other vulnerable Imperial outposts, human colonies or the home worlds of Terran-allied species. . . . Yes, Ardazir was surely planning to strike elsewhere within the Empire, and soon. Another one or two such blows, and the Imperial Navy *must* surrender Syrax to Merseia, turn inward and defend the mother planet. At which point—

*Not true that an army marches on its stomach,* thought Flandry. *It needs information even more than food. Marches on its head. Which, no doubt, is why the Imperial High Command has so many flat-heads.*

He chuckled. Bad as it was, the joke strengthened him. And he was going to need strength.

"Will you let me see?" asked Temulak in a small, broken voice.

"I will deprive you no longer of my beauty," said Flandry. He unhooded the rufous head and drew his wax plugs from the nose. Temulak blinked dazedly into smoke and one dull light. Flandry uncoupled the machines which had kept him alive. "You'll remain our guest, of course," he said. "If it turns out you prevaricated, back you go in the dark closet."

Temulak bristled. His teeth snapped together, missing the man's arm by a centimeter.

"Naughty!" Flandry stepped back. "For that, you can stay tied up a while."

Temulak snarled from the cot, "You gray-skinned hairless worm, if you think your *valkuza's* tricks will save you from the Black People—I myself will rip out your gullet and strangle you with your own bowels!"

"And foreclose my mortgage," said Flandry. He went out, closing the door behind him.

Bryce and Kit started. They had fallen asleep in their chairs. The hunter rubbed his eyes. "God o' the galaxy, you been at it a long time!" he exclaimed.

"Here." Flandry tossed him the tape spool. "This has to reach Admiral Walton's fleet. It's necessary, if not quite sufficient, for your liberation. Can do?"

"The enemy would pick up radio," said Bryce doubtfully. "We still got a few spaceships hid, but Kit's was the fastest. An' since then, too, the wolf space guard's been tightened till it creaks."

Flandry sighed. "I was afraid of that." He scribbled on a sheet of paper. "Here's a rough map to show you where my personal flitter is. D'you know this tune?" He whistled. "No? That proves you've a clean mind. Well, learn it." He rehearsed the Vixenite till he was satisfied. "Good. Approach the flitter whistling that, and Chives won't shoot you without investigation. Give him this note. It says for him to take the tape to Walton. If anything can run that blockade without collecting a missile, it's Chives in the *Hooligan*."

Kit suppressed a gasp. "But then you, Dominic— no escape—"

Flandry shrugged. "I'm much too tired to care about aught except a nice soft bed."

Bryce, sticking the spool under his tunic, grinned, "Whose?"

Kit stood as if struck.

Flandry nodded slightly at her. "That's the way of it." He glanced at his chrono. "Close to local midnight. Shove off, Bryce, lad. But stop by and tell Dr. Reineke to shift his apparatus and the prisoner elsewhere. It's always best to keep moving around, when you're being searched for. And nobody, except the pill peddler and whoever helps him, is to know where they stash Temulak next. All clear?"

"Dominic—" Kit closed her fists till the knuckles stood white. She stared down at the floor, he could only see her short bright hair.

He said gently, "I have to sleep or collapse, lass. I'll meet you at noon by the Rocket Fountain. I think we've a few private things to discuss."

She turned and fled upstairs.

Flandry departed too. The night sky was aflicker with aurora; he thought he could hear its ionic hiss in the city's blacked-out silence. Once he scrambled to a roof top and waited for an Ardazirho patrol to go by. Wan blue light glimmered off their metal and their teeth.

Judith made him welcome. "I've been so worried, darlin'—"

He considered her a while. Weariness dragged at him. But she had put out a late supper, with wine and a cold game bird, as she knew he liked it; and her hair glowed red by candlelight. Sleep be damned, Flandry decided. He might be permanently asleep tomorrow.

He did nap for a few morning hours, and went out before noon. Explorers' Plaza had been a gay scene once, where folk sat leisurely in the surrounding gardens, sipping coffee and listening to harp trees in the wind and watching life stream past. Now it was empty. The metal fountain itself, in the form of an ancient space rocket, still jetted many-colored heatless fires from its tail; but they seemed pale under the gloomy winter sky.

Flandry took out a cigarette, sat down on the fountain rim and waited. A few preliminary raindrops kissed his half lifted face.

A military truck careened out of a deserted street and ground to a halt. Three Ardazirho leaped from the cab. Kit was with them. She pointed at Flandry. Lightning blinked immediately overhead, and sudden thunder swamped her words. But the tone was vindictive.

"Halt, human!"

It must have been the only Anglic phrase any of the three invaders knew. They bayed it again and yet again as Flandry sprang to the plaza. He ducked and began to run, zigzagging.

No shots were fired. An Ardazirho yelped glee and opened the truck body. Wings snapped leathery. Flandry threw a glance behind. A score of meter-long snake bodies were streaming upward from the truck. They saw him, whistled and stooped.

Flandry ran. His heart began to pump, the wildness of irrational uncontrollable terror. The batsnakes reached him. He heard teeth click together behind his nape. A lean body coiled on his right arm. He jerked the limb up, frantic. Wings resisted him. Fangs needled into his flesh. The rest of the pack whirled and dove and whipped him with their tails.

He started to run again. The three Ardazirho followed, long bounds which took them over the ground faster than a man could speed. They howled, and there was laughter in their howling. The street was empty, resounding under boots. Shuttered windows looked down without seeing. Doors were closed and locked.

Flandry stopped. He spun around. His right arm was still cumbered. The left dove beneath his tunic. His needler came out. He aimed at the nearest of the laughing ruddy devils. A batsnake threw itself on his gun hand. It bit with trained precision, into the fingers. Flandry let the weapon fall. He snatched after the snake—to wring just one of their damned necks—!

It writhed free. Its reptile-like jaws grinned at him. Then the Ardazirho closed in.

## CHAPTER XII

MOST OF THE year, Vixen's northern half was simply desert, swamp, or prairie, where a quick vegetative life sprang up and animals that had been estivating crept from their burrows. The arctic even knew snow, when winter-long night had fallen. But in summer the snows melted to wild rivers, the rivers overflowed and became lakes, the lakes baked dry. Storms raged about the equator and into the southern hemisphere, as water precipitated again in cooler parts. Except for small seas dreary amidst salt flats, the north blistered arid. Fires broke loose, the pampas became barren again in a few red days. Under such erosive conditions, this land had no mountains. Most of it was plain, where dust and ash scoured on a furnace wind. In some places rose gnarled ranges, lifeless hills, twisted crags, arroyos carved by flash flood into huge earth scars.

The Ardazirho had established their headquarters in such a region, a little below the arctic circle. Thousands of lethal kilometers made it safe from human ground attack; the broken country was camouflage and protection from space-ships. Not that they tried to conceal their fortress absolutely. That would have been impossible. But it burrowed deep into the range and offered few specific targets.

Here and there Flandry saw a warship sitting insolently in the open, a missile emplacement, a detector station, a lookout tower black and lean against the blinding sky. Outer walls twisted through gullies and over naked ridges; Ardazirho sentries paced them, untroubled by dry cruel heat, blue-white hell-glare, pouring ultraviolet radiation. But mostly, the fortress went inside the hills, long vaulted tunnels where boots clashed and voices echoed from room to den-like room. Construction had followed standard dig-in methods: prodigal use of atomic energy to fuse the living rock into desired patterns, then swift robotic installation of the necessary mechanisms. But the layout was rougher, more tortuous, less private, than man or Merseian would have liked. The ancestral Ardazirho had laired in caves and hunted in packs.

Flandry was hustled into a small room equipped as a laboratory. A pair of warriors clamped him in place. A grizzled technician began to prepare instruments.

Often, in the next day or two, Flandry screamed. He couldn't help it. Electronic learning should not go that fast. But finally, sick and shaking, he could growl the Urdahu language. Indeed, he thought, the Ardazirho had been thoroughly briefed. They understood the human nervous system so well that they could stamp a new linguistic pattern on it in mere hours, and not drive the owner insane.

Not quite.

Flandry was led down endless booming halls. Their brilliant bluish fluorescence hurt his eyes, forcing him to squint. Even so, he watched what passed. It might be a truck load of ammunition, driven at crazy speed by a warrior who yelped curses at foot traffic. Or it might be a roomful of naked red-furred shapes; sprawled in snarling, quarrelsome fellow-ship; gambling with tetrahedral dice for stakes up to a year's slavery; watching a wrestling match which employed teeth and nails; testing nerve by standing up in turn against a wall while the rest threw axes. Or it might be a sort of chapel, where a single scarred fighter wallowed in pungent leaves before a great burning wheel. Or it might be a mess hall and a troop lying on fur rugs, bolting raw meat and howling in chorus with one who danced on a monstrous drumhead.

The man came at last to an office. This was also an

artificial cave, thick straw on the floor, gloom in the corners, a thin stream of water running down a groove in one wall. A big Ardazirho lay prone on a hairy dais, lifted on both elbows to a slanting desktop. He wore only a skirt of leather strips, a crooked knife and a very modern blaster. But the telescreen and intercom before him were also new, and Flandry's guards touched their black noses in his presence.

"Go," he said in the Urdahu. "Wait outside." The guards obeyed. He nodded at Flandry. "Be seated, if you wish."

The human lowered himself. He was still weak from what he had undergone, filthy, ill-fed, and ragged. Automatically he smoothed back his hair, and thanked human laziness, for its invention of long-lasting antibeard enzyme. He needed such morale factors.

His aching muscles grew tight. Things were in motion again.

"I am Svantozik of the Janneer Ya," said the rough voice. "I am told that you are Captain Dominic Flandry of Terran Naval Intelligence. You may consider my status approximately the same."

"As one colleague to another," husked Flandry, "will you give me a drink?"

"By all means." Svantozik gestured to the artesian stream.

Flandry threw him a reproachful look, but needed other things too badly to elaborate. "It would be a kindly deed, and one meriting my gratitude, if you provided me at once with dark lenses and cigarettes." The last word was perforce Anglic. He managed a grin. "Later I will tell you what further courtesies ought to be customary."

Svantozik barked laughter. "I expected your eyes would suffer," he said. "Here." He reached in the desk and tossed over a pair of green polarite goggles, doubtless taken off a Vixenite casualty. Flandry put them on and whistled relief. "Tobacco is forbidden," added Svantozik. "Only a species with half-dead scent organs could endure it."

"Oh, well. There was no harm in asking." Flandry hugged his knees and leaned back against the cave wall.

"None. Now, I wish to congratulate you on your daring exploits." Svantozik's smile looked alarming enough, but it seemed friendly. "We searched for your vessel, but it must have escaped the planet."

"Thanks," said Flandry, quite sincerely. "I was afraid you would have gotten there in time to blast it." He cocked his head. "In return . . . see here, my friend (literally: croucher-in-my-blind). When dealing with my species, it is usually better to discourage them. You should have claimed you had caught my boat before it could escape, manufacturing false evidence if necessary to convince me. That would make me much more liable to yield my will to yours."

"Oh, indeed?" Svantozik pricked up his ears. "Now among the Black People, the effect would be just opposite. Good news tends to relax us, make us grateful and amenable to its bearer. Bad tidings raise the quotient of defiance."

"Well, of course it is not that simple," said Flandry. "In breaking down the resistance of a man, the commonest technique is to chivvy him for a protracted time, and then halt the process, speak kindly to him—preferably, get someone else to do that."

"Ah." Svantozik drooped lids over his cold eyes. "Are you not being unwise in telling me this—if it is true?"

"It is textbook truth," said Flandry, "as I am sure whatever race has instructed you in the facts about Terra's Empire will confirm. I am revealing no secret. But as you must be aware, textbooks have little value in practical matters. There is always the subtlety of the individual, which eludes anything except direct intuition based on wide, intimate experience. And you, being nonhuman, cannot ever have such an experience of men."

"True." The long head nodded. "In fact, I remember now reading somewhat of the human trait you mention . . . but there was so much else to learn, prior to the Great Hunt we are now on, that it had slipped my memory. So you tantalize me with a fact I could use— if I were on your side!" A sudden deep chuckle cracked in the ruffed throat. "I like you, Captain, the Sky Cave eat me if I do not."

Flandry smiled back. "We could have fun. But what are your intentions toward me now?"

"To learn what I can. For example, whether or not you were concerned in the murder of four warriors in Garth and the abduction of a fifth, not long ago. The informant who led us to you has used hysterics—real or simulated—to escape detailed questioning so far. Since the captured Ardazirho was a Clanmaster, and therefore possessed of valuable information, I suspect you had a hand in this."

"I swear upon the Golden Ass of Apuleius I did not."

"What is that?"

"One of our most revered books."

" 'The Powers only hunt at night,' " quoted Svantozik. "In other words, oaths are cheap. I personally do not wish to hurt you unduly, being skeptical of the value of torture anyhow. And I know that officers like you are immunized to the so-called truth sera. Therefore, reconditioning would be necessary; a long, tedious process, the answers stale when finally you wanted to give them, and you of little further value to us or yourself." He shrugged. "But I am going back to Ardazir before long, to report and await reassignment. I know who will succeed me here; an officer quite anxious to practice some of the techniques which we have been told are effective on Terrans. I recommend you co-operate with me, instead."

*This must be one of their crack field operatives,* thought Flandry, growing cold. *He did the basic Intelligence work on Vixen. Now, with Vixen in hand, he'll be sent to do the same job when the next Terran planet is attacked. Which will be soon!*

Flandry slumped. "Very well," he said in a dull tone. "I captured Temulak."

"Ha!" Svantozik crouched all-fours on the dais. The fur stood up along his spine, the iron-colored eyes burned. "Where is he now?"

"I do not know. As a precaution, I had him moved elsewhere, and did not inquire the place."

"Wise." Svantozik relaxed. "What did you get from him?"

"Nothing. He did not crack."

Svantozik stared at Flandry. "I doubt that," he said. "Not

that I scorn Temulak—a brave one—but you are an extraordinary specimen of a civilization older and more learned than mine. It would be strange if you had not—"

Flandry sat up straight. His laughter barked harsh. "'Extraordinary?" he cried bitterly. "I suppose so . . . the way I allowed myself to be caught like a cub!"

" 'No ground is free of possible pits,' " murmured Svantozik. He brooded a while. Presently, "Why did the female betray you? She went to our headquarters, declared you were a Terran agent, and led our warriors to your meeting place. What had she to gain?"

"I don't know," groaned Flandry. "What difference does it make? She is wholly yours now, you know. The very fact she aided you once gives you the power to make her do it again—lest you denounce her to her own people." Svantozik nodded, grinning. "What do her original motives matter?" The man sagged back and picked at the straw.

"I am interested," said Svantozik. "Perhaps the same process may work again, on other humans."

"No." Flandry shook his head in a stunned way. "This was personal. I suppose she thought I had betrayed her first— Why am I telling you this?"

"I have been informed that you Terrans often have strong feelings about individuals of the opposite sex," said Svantozik. "I was told it will occasionally drive you to desperate, meaningless acts."

Flandry passed a tired hand across his brow. "Forget it," he mumbled. "Just be kind to her. You can do that much, can you not?"

"As a matter of fact—" Svantozik broke off. He sat for a moment, staring at emptiness.

"*Great unborn planets*!" he whispered.

"What?" Flandry didn't look up.

"No matter," said Svantozik hastily. "Ah, am I right in assuming there was a reciprocal affection on your part?"

"It is no concern of yours!" Flandry sat up and shouted it. "I will hear no more! Say what else you will, but keep your filthy snout out of my own life!"

"So," breathed Svantozik. "Yes-s-s-s. . . . Well, then, let us discuss other things."

He hammered at Flandry a while, not with quite the ruthlessness the human had shown Temulak. Indeed, he revealed a kind of chivalry; there was respect, fellow feeling, even an acrid liking in him for this man whose soul he hunted. Once or twice Flandry managed to divert the conversation—they spoke briefly of alcoholic drinks and riding animals; they traded some improper jokes, similar in both cultures.

Nevertheless, Svantozik hunted. It was a rough few hours.

At last Flandry was taken away. He was too worn to notice very much, but the route did seem devious. He was finally pushed into a room, not unlike Svantozik's office, save that it had human-type furniture and illumination. The door clashed behind him.

Kit stood waiting.

## CHAPTER XIII

FOR A MOMENT he thought she would scream. Then, very quickly, her eyes closed. She opened them again. They remained closed. She opened them again. They remained dry, as if all her tears had been spent. She took a step toward him.

"Oh, God, Kit," he croaked.

Her arms closed about his neck. He held her to him. His own gaze flickered around the room, until it found a small human-made box with a few controls which he recognized. He nodded to himself, ever so faintly, and drew an uneven breath. But he was still uncertain.

"Dominic, darlin'—" Kit's mouth sought his.

He stumbled to the bunk, sat down and covered his face. "Don't he whispered. "I can't take much more."

The girl sat down beside him. She laid her head on his shoulder. He felt how she trembled. But the words came in glorious anticlimax, "That debuggin' unit is perfectly good, Dominic."

He wanted to lean back and shout with sudden uproarious mirth. He wanted to kick his heels and thumb his nose and turn handsprings across the cell. But he held himself in, letting only a rip of laughter come from lips which he hid against her cheek.

He had more than half expected Svantozik to provide a bug-scrambler. Only with the sure knowledge that any listening devices were being negated by electronic and sound-wave interference, would even a cadet of Intelligence relax and speak freely. He suspected, though, that a hidden lens was conveying a silent image. They could talk, but both of them must continue to pantomine.

"How's it been, Kit?" he asked. "Rough?"

She nodded, not play-acting her misery at all. "But I haven't had to give any names," she gulped. "Not yet."

"Let's hope you don't," said Flandry.

*He had told her in the hurricane cellar—how many centuries ago?— "This is picayune stuff. I'm not doing what any competent undercover agent couldn't; what a score of Walton's men will be trying as soon as they can be smuggled here. I've something crazier in mind. Quite likely it'll kill us, but then again it might strike a blow worth whole fleets. Are you game, kid? It means the risk of death, or torture, or lifelong slavery on a foreign planet. What you'll find worst, though, is the risk of having to sell out your own comrades, name them to the enemy, so he will keep confidence in you. Are you brave enough to sacrifice twenty lives for a world? I believe you are—but it's as cruel a thing as I could ask of any living creature."*

"They brought me straight here," said Kit, holding him. "I don't think they know quite what to make o' me. A few minutes ago, one o' them came hotfootin' here with the scrambler an' orders for me to treat you—" a slow flush went over her face—"kindly. To get information from you, if I could, by any means that seemed usable."

Flandry waved a fist in melodramatic despair, while out of a contorted face his tone came levelly, "I expected something like this. I led Svantozik, the local snooper-in-chief, to think that gentle treatment from one of my own species, after a hard grilling from him, might break me down. Especially if you were the one in question. Svantozik isn't stupid at all, but he's dealing with an alien race, us, whose psychology he knows mainly from sketchy secondhand accounts. I've an advantage; the Ardazirho are new to me, but I've spent a lifetime dealing with all shapes and sizes of other species. Already I see what the Ardazirho have in common with several peoples whom I hornswoggled in the past."

The girl bit her lip to hold it steady. She looked around the stone-walled room, and he knew she thought of kilometers of tunnel, ramparts and guns, wolfish hunters, and the desert beyond where men could not live. Her words fell thin and frightened, "What are we goin' to do now, Dominic? You never told me what you planned."

"Because I didn't know," he replied. "Once here, I'd have to play by ear. Fortunately, my confidence in my own ability to land on my feet approaches pure conceit, or would if I had any faults. We're not doing badly, Kit. I've learned their principal language, and you've been smuggled into their ranks."

"They don't trust me yet."

"No. I didn't expect they would—very much. . . . But let's carry on our visual performance. I wouldn't flipflop over to the enemy side just because you're here, Kit; but I am badly shaken, I lose discretion and ordinary carefulness. Svantozik will accept that."

He gathered her back to him. She responded hungrily. He felt so much of himself return to his abused being, that his brain began to spark, throwing up schemes and inspecting them, discarding them and generating new ones, like a pyrotechnic display, like merry hell.

He said at last, while she quivered on his lap, "I think I have a notion. We'll have to play things as they lie, and pre-arrange a few signals, but here's what we'll try for." He felt her stiffen in his embrace. "Why, what's the matter?"

She asked, low and bitter: "Were you thinkin' o' your work all the time—just now?"

"Not that alone." He permitted himself the briefest grin. "Or, rather, I enjoyed my work immensely."

"But still—Oh, never mind. Go on." She slumped.

Flandry scowled. But he dared not stop for side issues. He said, "Tell Svantozik, or whoever deals with you, that you played remorseful in my presence, but actually you hate my inwards and my outwards too, because—uh—"

"Judith!" she snarled.

He had the grace to blush. "I suppose that's as plausible a reason as any, at least in Ardazirho eyes."

"Or human. If you knew how close I was to— No. Go on."

"Well, tell the enemy that you told me you'd betrayed me in a fit of pique, and now you regretted it. And I, being wildly in love with you—which again is highly believable—" She gave his predictable gallantry no response whatsoever. "I told you there was a possible escape for you. I said this: The Ardazirho are under the impression that Ymir is behind them. Actually, Ymir leans toward Terra, since we are more peace-minded and therefore less troublesome. The Ymirites are willing to help us in small ways; we keep this fact secret because now and then it saves us in emergencies. If I could only set a spaceship's signal to a certain recognition pattern, you could try to steal that ship. The Ardazirho would assume you headed for Walton's fleet, and line out after you in that direction. So you could give them the slip, reach Ogre, transmit the signal pattern, and request transportation to safety in a force-bubble ship."

Her eyes stretched wide with terror. "But if Svantozik hears that—an' 'tisn't true—"

"He won't know it's false till he's tried, will he?" answered

Flandry cheerfully. "If I lied, it isn't your fault. In fact, since you hastened to tattle, even about what looked like an escape for you, it'll convince him you're a firm collaborationist."

"But—no, Dominic. 'Tis . . . I don't dare—"

"Don't hand me that, Kit. You're one girl in ten to the tenth, and there's nothing you won't dare."

Then she began to sob.

After she had gone, Flandry spent a much less happy time waiting. He could still only guess how his enemy would react; an experienced human would probably not be deceived, and Svantozik's ignorance of human psychology might not be as deep as hoped. Flandry swore and tried to rest. The weariness of the past days was gray upon him.

When his cell door opened, he sprang up with a jerkiness that told him how thin his nerves were worn.

Svantozik stood there, four guards poised behind. The Ardazirho officer flashed teeth in a grin. "Good hunting, Captain," he greeted. "Is your den comfortable?"

"It will do," said Flandry, "until I can get one provided with a box of cigars, a bottle of whiskey, and a female."

"The female, at least, I tried to furnish," riposted Svantozik.

Flandry added in his suavest tone, "Oh, yes, I should also like a rug of Ardazirho skin."

One of the guards snarled. Svantozik chuckled. "I too have a favor to ask, Captain," he said. "My brothers in the engineering division are interested in modifying a few spaceships to make them more readily usable by humans. You understand how such differences as the location of the thumb, or that lumbar conformation which makes it more comfortable for us to lie prone on the elbows than sit, have influenced the design of our control panels. A man would have trouble steering an Ardazirho craft. Yet necessarily, in the course of time, if the Great Hunt succeeds and we acquire human subjects—we will find occasion for some of them to pilot some of our vehicles. The Kittredge female, for example, could profitably have a ship of her own, since we anticipate usefulness in her as a go-between among us and the human colonists here. If you would help her—simply in checking over one of our craft, and drawing up suggestions—"

Flandry grew rigid. "Why should I help you at all?" he said through clenched jaws.

Svantozik shrugged. "It is very minor assistance. We could do it ourselves, But it may pass the time for you." Wickedly, "I am not at all sure that good treatment, rather than abuse, may not be the way to break down a man. Also, Captain, if you must have a rationalization, think; here is a chance to examine one of our vessels close up. If later, somehow, you escape, your own service would be interested in what you saw."

Flandry stood a moment, altogether quiet. Thought lanced through him: *Kit told. Svantozik naturally prefers me not to know what she did tell. So he makes up this story—offers me what he hopes I'll think is a God-sent opportunity to arrange for Kit's escape—*

He said aloud, urbanely, "You are most kind, my friend of-Janneer. But Miss Kittredge and I could not feel at ease with ugly guards like yours drooling over our shoulders."

He got growls from two warriors that time. Svantozik hushed them. "That is easily arranged," he said. "The guards can stay out of the control turret."

"Excellent. Then, if you have some human-made tools—"

They went down hollow corridors, past emplacements where artillery slept like nested dinosaurs, across the furious artic day, and so to a spaceship near the outworks. Through goggles, the man studied her fiercely gleaming shape. About equivalent to a Terran Comet class. Fast, lightly armed, a normal complement of fifteen or so, but one could handle her if need be.

The naked hills beyond wavered in heat. When he had stepped through the airlock, he felt dizzy from that brief exposure.

Svantozik stopped at the turret companionway. "Proceed," he invited cordially. "My warriors will wait here until you wish to return—at which time you and the female will come dine with me and I shall provide Terran delicacies." Mirth crossed his eyes. "Of course, the engines have been temporarily disconnected."

"Of course," bowed Flandry.

Kit met him as he shut the turret door. Her fingers closed cold on his arm. "Now what'll we do?" she gasped.

"Easy, lass." He disengaged her. "I don't see a bug scrambler here." *Remember, Svantozik thinks I think you are still loyal to me. Play it, Kit, don't forget, or we're both done!* "There are four surly-looking guards slouched below," he said. "I don't imagine Svantozik will waste his own valuable time in their company. A direct bug to the office of someone who knows Anglic is more efficient. Consider me making gestures at you, O great unseen audience. But is anyone else aboard, d'you know?"

"N-no—" Her eyes asked him, through fear, *Have you forgotten? Are you alerting them to your plan?*

Flandry wandered past the navigation table to the main radio transceiver. "I don't want to risk someone getting officious," he murmured. "You see, I'd first like a peek at their communication system. It's the easiest thing to modify, if any alterations are needed. And it could look bad, unseen audience, if we were surprised at what is really a harmless inspection." *I trust,* he thought with a devil's inward laughter, *that they don't know I know they know I'm actually supposed to install a password circuit for Kit.*

It was the sort of web he loved. But he remembered, as a cold tautening, that a bullet was still the ultimate simplicity which clove all webs.

He took the cover off and began probing. He could not simply have given Kit the frequencies and wave shapes in a recognition signal, because Ardazirho equipment would not be built just like Terran, nor calibrated in metric units. He must examine an actual set, dismantle parts, test them with oscilloscope and static meters—and, surreptitiously, modify it so that the required pattern would be emitted when a single hidden circuit was closed.

She watched him, as she should if she expected him to

believe this was her means of escape. And doubtless the Ardazirho spy watched too, over a bugscreen. When Flandry's job was done, it would be Svantozik who took this ship to Ogre, generated the signal, and saw what happened.

Because the question of whose side the Ymirite Dispersal truly was on, overrode everything else. If Flandry had spoken truth to Kit, the lords of Urdahu must be told without an instant's pause.

The man proceeded, making up a pattern as if Ymir really did favor Terra. Half an hour later he resealed the unit. Then he spent another hour ostentatiously strolling around the turret examining all controls.

"Well," he said at last, "we might as well go home, Kit."

He saw the color leave her face. She knew what that sentence meant. But she nodded. "Let's," she whispered.

Flandry bowed her through the door. As she came down the companionway, the guards at its base got up. Their weapons aimed past her, covering Flandry, who strolled with a tigerish leisure.

Kit pushed through the line of guards. Flandry, still on the companionway, snatched at his pocket. The four guns leaped to focus on him. He laughed and raised empty hands. "I only wanted to scratch an itch," he called.

Kit slipped a knife from the harness of one guard and stabbed him in the ribs.

Flandry dove into the air. A bolt crashed past him, scorching his tunic. He struck the deck with flexed knees and bounced. Kit had already snatched the rifle from the yelling warrior she had wounded. It thundered in her hand, point-blank. Another Ardazirho dropped. Flandry knocked aside the gun of a third. The fourth enemy had whipped around toward Kit. His back was to Flandry. The man raised the blade of his hand and brought it down again, chop to the skull-base. He heard neckbones splinter. The third guard sprang back, seeking room to shoot. Kit blasted him open. The first one, stabbed, on his knees, reached for a dropped rifle. Flandry kicked him in the larynx.

"Starboard lifeboat!" he rasped.

He clattered back into the turret. If the Ardazirho watcher had left the bugscreen by now, he had a few minutes' grace. Otherwise, a nuclear shell would probably write his private doomsday. He snatched up the navigator's manual and sprang out again.

Kit was already in the lifeboat. Its small engine purred, warming up. Flandry plunged through the lock, dogged it behind him. "I'll fly," he panted. "I'm more used to non-Terran panels. You see if you can find some bailing-out equipment. We'll need it."

Where the devil was the release switch? The bugwatcher had evidently quit in time, but any moment now he would start to wonder why Flandry and Party weren't yet out of the spaceship—

There! He slapped down a lever. A hull panel opened. Harsh sunlight poured through the boat's viewscreen. Flandry glanced over its controls. Basically like those he had just studied. He touched the *Escape* button. The engine yelled. The boat sprang from its mother ship, into the sky.

Flandry aimed southward. He saw the fortress whirl dizzily away, fall below the horizon. And still no pursuit, not even a homing missile. They must be too dumfounded. It wouldn't last, of course. . . . He threw back his head and howled out all his bottled-up laughter, great gusts of it to fill the cabin and echo over the scream of split atmosphere.

"What are you doin'?" Kit's voice came faint and frantic. "We can't escape this way. Head spaceward before they overhaul us!"

Flandry wiped his eyes. "Excuse me," he said. "I was laughing while I could." Soberly, "With the blockade, and a slow vessel never designed for human steering, we'd not climb 10,000 kilometers before they nailed us. What we're going to do is bail out and let the boat continue on automatic. With luck, they'll pursue it so far before catching up that they'll have no prayer of backtracking us. With still more luck, they'll blow the boat up and assume we were destroyed too."

"Bail out?" Kit looked down at a land of stones and

blowing ash. The sky above was like molten steel. "Into that?" she whispered.

"If they do realize we jumped," said Flandry, "I trust they'll figure we perished in the desert. A natural conclusion, I'm sure, since our legs aren't so articulated that we can wear Ardazirho spacesuits." He grew grimmer than she had known him before. "I've had to improvise all along the way. Quite probably I've made mistakes, Kit, which will cost us a painful death. But if so, I'm hoping we won't die for naught."

## CHAPTER XIV

EVEN RIDING a grav repulsor down, Flandry felt how the air smote him with heat. When he struck the ground and rolled over, it burned his skin.

He climbed up, already ill. Through his goggles, he saw Kit rise. Dust veiled her, blown on a furnace wind. The desert reached in withered soil and bony crags for a few kilometers beyond her, then the heat-haze swallowed vision. The northern horizon seemed incandescent, impossible to look at.

Thunder banged in the wake of the abandoned lifeboat. Flandry stumbled toward the girl. She leaned on him. "I'm sorry," she said. "I think I twisted an ankle."

"And scorched it, too, I see. Come on lass, not far now."

They groped over tumbled gray boulders. The weather monitor tower rippled before their eyes, like a skeleton seen through water. The wind blasted and whined. Flandry felt his skin prickle with ultraviolet and bake dry as he walked. The heat began to penetrate his boot soles.

They were almost at the station when a whistle cut through the air. Flandry lifted aching eyes. Four torpedo shapes went overhead, slashing from horizon to horizon in seconds. The Ardazirho, in pursuit of an empty lifeboat. If they had seen the humans below— No. They were gone. Flandry tried to grin, but it split his lips too hurtfully.

The station's equipment huddled in a concrete shack beneath the radio transmitter tower. The shade, when they had staggered through the door, was like all hopes of heaven. Flandry uncorked a water bottle. That was all he had dared take, out of the spaceboat supplies; alien food was liable to have incompatible proteins. His throat was too much like a mummy's to talk, but he offered Kit the flask and she gulped thirstily. When he had also swigged, he felt a little better.

"Get to work, wench," he said. "Isn't it lucky you're in Vixen's weather engineering department, so you knew where to find a station and what to do when we got there?"

"Go on," she tried to laugh. It was a rattling in her mouth. "You built your idea arou' the fact. Let's see, now, they keep tools in a locker at every unit—" She stopped. The shadow in this hut was so deep, against the fury seen through one little window, that she was almost invisible to him. "I can tinker with the sender, easily enough," she said. Slow terror rose in her voice. "Sure, I can make it 'cast your message, 'stead o' telemeterin' weather data. But . . . I just now get to thinkin' . . . s'pose an Ardazirho reads it? Or s'pose nobody does? I don't know if my service is even bein' manned now. We could wait here, an' wait, an'—"

"Easy." Flandry came behind her, laid his hands on her shoulders and squeezed. "Anything's possible. But I think the chances favor us. The Ardazirho can hardly spare personnel for something so routine and, to them, unimportant, as weather adjustment. At the same time, the human engineers are very probably still on the job. Humanity always continues as much in the old patterns as possible, people report to their usual work, hell may open but the city will keep every lawn mowed. . . . Our real gamble is that whoever spots our call will have the brains, and the courage and loyalty, to act on it."

She leaned against him a moment. "An' d'you think there's a way for us to be gotten out o' here, under the enemy's nose?"

An obscure pain twinged in his soul. "I know it's unfair, Kit," he said. "I myself am a hardened sinner and this is my job and so on, but it isn't right to hazard all the fun and love and accomplishment waiting for you. It must be done, though. My biggest hope was always to steal a navigation manual. Don't you understand, it will tell us where Ardazir lies!"

"I know." Her sigh was a small sound almost lost in the boom of dry hot wind beyond the door. "We'd better start work."

While she opened the transmitter and cut out the meter circuits, Flandry recorded a message, a simple plea to contact Emil Bryce and arrange the rescue from Station 938 of two humans with vital material for Admiral Walton. How that was to be done, he had no clear idea himself. A Vixenite aircraft would have little chance of getting this far north undetected and undestroyed. A radio message—no, too easily intercepted, unless you had very special apparatus— a courier to the fleet—and if that was lost, another and another—

When she had finished, Kit reached for the second water bottle. "Better not," said Flandry. "We've a long wait."

"I'm dehydrated," she husked.

"Me too. But we've no salt; heat stroke is a real threat. Drinking as little as possible will stretch our survival time. Why the devil aren't these places air conditioned and stocked with rations?"

"No need for it. They just get routine inspection . . . at midwinter in these parts." Kit sat down on the one little bench. Flandry joined her. She leaned into the curve of his arm. A savage gust trembled in the hut walls, the window was briefly blackened with flying grit.

"Is Ardazir like this?" she wondered. "Then 'tis a real hell for those devils to come from."

"Oh, no," answered Flandry. "Temulak said their planet

has a sane orbit. Doubtless it's warmer than Terra, on the average, but we could stand the temperature in most of its climatic zones, I'm sure. A hot star, emitting strongly in the UV, would split water molecules and kick the free hydrogen into space before it could recombine. The ozone layer would give some protection to the hydrosphere, but not quite enough. So Ardazir must be a good deal drier than Terra, with seas rather than oceans. At the same time, judging from the muscular strength of the natives, as well as the fact they don't mind Vixen's air pressure, Ardazir must be somewhat bigger. Surface gravity of one-point-five, maybe. That would retain an atmosphere similar to ours, in spite of the sun."

He paused. Then, "They aren't fiends, Kit. They're fighters and hunters. Possibly they've a little less built-in kindliness than our species. But I'm not even sure about that. We were a rambunctious lot, too, a few centuries ago. We may well be again, when the Long Night has come and it's root, hog, or die. As a matter of fact, the Ardazirho aren't even one people. They're a whole planetful of races and cultures. The Urdahu conquered the rest only a few years ago. That's why you see all those different clothes on them—concession to parochialism, like an ancient Highland regiment. And I'll give odds that in spite of all their successes, the Urdahu are not too well liked at home. Theirs is a very new empire, imposed by overwhelming force; it could be split again, if we used the right tools. I feel almost sorry for them, Kit. They're the dupes of someone else—and Lord, what a someone that is! What a genius!"

He stopped, because the relentless waterless heat had shriveled his gullet. The girl said, low and bitter, "Go on. Sympathize with Ardazir an' admire the artistry o' this X who's behind it all. You're a professional, too. But my kind o' people has to do the dyin'."

"I'm sorry." He ruffled her hair.

"You still haven't tol' me whether you think we'll be rescued alive."

"I don't know." He tensed himself until he could add, "I doubt it. I expect it'll take days, and we can only hold out for hours. But if the ship comes—no, damn it, *when* the ship comes!—that pilot book will be here."

"Thanks for bein' honest, Dominic," she said. "Thanks for everything."

He kissed her, with enormous gentleness.

After that they waited.

The sun sank. A short night fell. It brought little relief, the wind still scourging, the northern sky still aflame. Kit tossed in a feverish daze beside Flandry. He himself could no longer think very clearly. He had hazy recollections of another white night in high-latitude summer—but that had been on Terra, on a cool upland meadow of Norway, and there had been another blonde girl beside him—her lips were like roses. . . .

This whistling down the sky, earth-shaking thump of a recklessly fast landing, feet that hurried over blistering rock and hands that hammered on the door, scarcely reached through the charred darkness of Flandry's mind. But when the door crashed open and the wind blasted in, he swam up through waves of pain. And the thin face of Chives waited to meet him.

"Here, sir. Sit up. If I may take the liberty—"

"You green bastard," croaked Flandry out of nightmare, "I ordered you to—"

"Yes, sir. I delivered your tape. But after that, it seemed advisable to slip back and stay in touch with Mr. Bryce. Easy there, sir, if you please. We can run the blockade with little trouble. Really, sir, did you think *natives* could bar your own personal spacecraft? I shall prepare medication for the young lady, and tea is waiting in your stateroom."


## CHAPTER XV

FLEET Admiral Sir Thomas Walton was a big man, with gray hair and bleak faded eyes. He seldom wore any of his decorations, and visited Terra only on business. No sculp, but genes and war and unshed tears, when he watched his men die and then watched the Imperium dribble away what they had gained, had carved his face. Kit thought him the handsomest man she had ever met. But in her presence, his tongue locked with the shyness of an old bachelor. He called her Miss Kittredge, assigned her a private cabin in his flagship, and found excuses to avoid the officers' mess where she ate.

She was given no work, save keeping out of the way. Lonely young lieutenants buzzed about her, doing their best to charm and amuse. But Flandry was seldom aboard the dreadnaught.

The fleet orbited in darkness, among keen sardonic stars. Little could actively be done. Ogre must be watched, where the giant planet crouched an enigma. The Ardazirho force did not seek battle, but stayed close to Vixen where ground support was available and where captured robofactories daily swelled its strength. Now and then the Terrans made forays. But Walton hung back from a decisive test. He could still win—*if* he used his whole strength and if Ogre stayed neutral. But Vixen, the prize, would be a tomb.

Restless and unhappy, Walton's men muttered in their ships.

After three weeks, Captain Flandry was summoned to the admiral. He whistled relief. "Our scout must have reported back," he said to his assistant. "Now maybe they'll take me off this damned garbage detail."

The trouble was, he alone had been able to speak Urdahu. There were a few hundred Ardazirho prisoners, taken off disabled craft by boarding parties. But the officers had destroyed all navigational clues and died, with the ghastly gallantry of preconditioning. None of the enlisted survivors knew Anglic, or co-operated with the Terran linguists. Flandry had passed on his command of their prime tongue, electronically; but not wishing to risk his sanity again, he had done it at the standard easy pace. The rest of each day had been spent interrogating—a certain percentage of prisoners were vulnerable to it in their own language. Now, two other humans possessed Urdahu; enough of a seedbed. But until the first spies sent to Ardazir itself got back, Flandry had been left on the grilling job. Sensible, but exhausting and deadly dull.

He hopped eagerly into a grav scooter and rode from the Intelligence ship to the dreadnaught. It was Nova class; its hull curved over him, monstrous as a mountain, guns raking the Milky Way. Otherwise he saw only stars, the distant sun Cerulia, the black nebula. Hard to believe that hundreds of ships, with the unchained atom in their magazines, prowled for a million kilometers around.

He entered the Nr. 7 lock and strode quickly toward the flag office. A scarlet cloak billowed behind him; his tunic was peacock blue, his trousers like snow, tucked into half-boots of authentic Cordovan leather. The angle of his cap was an outrage to all official dignity. He felt like a boy released from school.

"Dominic!"

Flandry stopped. "Kit!" he whooped.

She ran down the corridor to meet him, a small lonely figure in brief Terran dress. Her hair was still a gold helmet, but he noted she was thinner. He put hands on her shoulders and held her at arm's length. "The better to see you with," he laughed. And then, soberly, "Tough?"

"Lonesome," she said. "Empty. Nothin' to do but worry." She pulled away from him. "No, darn it, I hate people who feel sorry for themselves. I'm all right, Dominic." She looked down at the deck and knuckled one eye.

"Come on!" he said.

"Hm? Dominic, where are you goin'? I can't—I mean—"

Flandry slapped her in the most suitable place and hustled her along the hall. "You're going to sit in on this! It'll give you something to hope for. March!"

The guard outside Walton's door was shocked. "Sir, my orders were to admit only you."

"One side, junior." Flandry picked up the marine by the gun belt and set him down a meter away. "The young lady is my portable expert on hypersquidgeronics. Also, she's pretty." He closed the door in the man's face.

Admiral Walton started behind his desk. "What's this, Captain?"

"I thought she could pour beer for us," burbled Flandry.

"I don't—" began Kit helplessly. "I didn't mean to—"

"Sit down." Flandry pushed her into a corner chair. "After all, sir, we might need first-hand information about Vixen." His eyes clashed with Walton's. "I think she's earned a ringside seat," he added.

The admiral sat unmoving a moment. Then his mouth crinkled. "You're incorrigible," he said. "And spare me that stock answer, 'No, I'm Flandry.' Very well, Miss Kittredge. You understand this is under top security. Captain Flandry, you know Commander Sugimoto."

Flandry shook hands with the other Terran, who had been in charge of the first sneak expedition to Ardazir. They sat down. Flandry started a cigarette. "D'you find the place all right?" he asked.

"No trouble," said Sugimoto. "Once you'd given me the correlation between their astronomical tables and ours, and explained the number system, it was elementary. Their star's not in our own catalogues, because it's on the other side of that dark nebula and there's never been any exploration that way. So you've saved us maybe a year of search. Incidentally, when the war's over the scientists will be interested in the nebula. Seen from the other side, it's faintly luminous; a proto-sun. No one ever suspected that Population One got *that* young right in Sol's own galactic neighborhood! Must be a freak, though."

Flandry stiffened. "What's the matter?" snapped Walton.

"Nothing, sir. Or maybe something. I don't know. Go on, Commander."

"No need to repeat in detail," said Walton. "You'll see the full report. Your overall picture of Ardazirho conditions, gained from your interrogations, is accurate. The sun is an A4 dwarf—actually no more than a dozen parsecs from here. The planet is terrestroid, biggish, rather dry, quite mountainous, three satellites. From all indications—you know the techniques, sneak landings, long-range telescopic spying, hidden cameras, random samples—the Urdahu hegemony is recent and none too stable."

"One of our xenologists spotted what he swore was a typical rebellion," said Sugimoto. "To me, his films are merely a lot of red hairy creatures in one kind of clothes, firing with gunpowder weapons at a modern-looking fortress where they wear different clothes. The sound track won't mean a thing till your boys translate for us. But the xenologist says there are enough other signs to prove it's the uprising of a backward tribe against more civilized conquerors."

"A chance, then, to play them off against each other," nodded Flandry. "Of course, before we can hope to do that, Intelligence must first gather a lot more information. Advertisement."

"Have you anything to add, Captain?" asked Walton. "Anything you learned since your last progress report?"

"No, sir," said Flandry. "It all hangs together pretty well. Except, naturally, the main question. The Urdahu couldn't have invented all the modern paraphernalia that gave them control of Ardazir. Not that fast. They were still in the early nuclear age, two decades ago. Somebody supplied them, taught them, and sent them out a-conquering. Who?"

"Ymir," said Walton flatly. "Our problem is, are the Ymirites working independently, or as allies of Merseia?"

"Or at all?" murmured Flandry.

"Hell and thunder! The Ardazirho ships and heavy equipment have Ymirite lines. The governor of Ogre ties up half our strength simply by refusing to speak. A Jovian colonist tried to murder you when you were on an official mission, didn't he?"

"The ships could be made that way on purpose, to mislead us," said Flandry. "You know the Ymirites are not a courteous race; even if they were, what difference would it make, since we can't investigate them in detail? As for my little brush with Horx—"

He stopped. "Commander," he said slowly, "I've learned there are Jovoid planets in the system of Ardazir. Is any of them colonized?"

"Not as far as I could tell," said Sugimoto. "Of course, with that hot sun . . . I mean, we wouldn't colonize Ardazir, so Ymir—"

"The sun doesn't make a lot of difference when atmosphere gets that thick," said Flandry. "My own quizzing led me to believe there are no Ymirite colonies anywhere in the region overrun by Ardazir. Don't you think, if they had interests there at all, they'd *live* there?"

"Not necessarily." Walton's fist struck the desk. "Everything's 'not necessarily,' " he growled, like a baited lion. "We're fighting in a fog. If we made an all-out attack anywhere, we'd expose ourselves to possible Ymirite action. This fleet is stronger than the Ardazirho force around Vixen—but weaker than the entire fleet of the whole Ardazirho realm— yet if we pulled in reinforcements from Syrax, Merseia would gobble up the Cluster! But we can't hang around here forever, either, waiting for somebody's next move!"

He stared at his big knobbly hands. "We'll send more spies to Ardazir," he rumbled. "Of course some'll get caught, and then Ardazir will know we know, and they'll really exert themselves against us. . . . By God, maybe the one thing to do is smash them here at Vixen, immediately, and then go straight to Ardazir and hope enough of our ships survive long enough to sterilize the whole hell-planet!"

Kit leaped to her feet. "No!" she screamed.

Flandry forced her down again. Walton looked at her with eyes full of anguish. "I'm sorry," he mumbled. "I know it would be the end of Vixen. I don't want to be a butcher at Ardazir either . . . all their little cubs, who never heard about war— But what can I do?"

"Wait," said Flandry. "I have a hunch."

Silence fell, layer by layer, until the cabin grew thick with it. Finally Walton asked, most softly, "What is it, Captain?"

Flandry stared past them all. "Maybe nothing," he said. "Maybe much. An expression some of the Ardazirho use: the Sky Cave. It's some kind of black hole. Certain of their religions make it the entrance to hell. Could it be—I remember my friend Svantozik too. I surprised him, and he let out

an oath which was not stock. *Great unborn planets.* Svantozik
ranks high. He knows more than any other Ardazirho we've
met. It's little enough to go on, but . . . can you spare me a
flotilla, Admiral?"

"Probably not," said Walton. "And it couldn't sneak off.
One ship at a time, yes, we can get that out secretly. But
several— The enemy would detect their wake, notice which
way they were headed, and wonder. Or wouldn't that matter
in this case?"

"I'm afraid it would." Flandry paused. "Well, sir, can
you lend me a few men? I'll take my own flitter. If I'm not
back soon, do whatever seems best."

He didn't want to go. It seemed all too likely that the myth
was right and the Sky Cave led to hell. But Walton sat
watching him, Walton who was one of the last brave and
wholly honorable men in all Terra's Empire. And Kit
watched him, too.

# CHAPTER XVI

HE WOULD have departed at once, but a stroke of luck—
*about time,* he thought ungratefully—made him decide to
wait another couple of days. He spent them on the *Hooligan,*
not telling Kit he was still with the fleet. If she knew he had
leisure, he would never catch up on some badly needed sleep.

The fact was that the Ardazirho remained unaware that
any human knew their language, except a few prisoners and
the late Dominic Flandry. So they were sending all messages
in clear. By now Walton had agents on Vixen, working with
the underground, equipped to communicate undetected with

his fleet. Enemy transmissions were being monitored with growing thoroughness. Flandry remembered that Svantozik had been about to leave, and requested a special lookout for any information on this subject. A scanner was adjusted to spot that name on a recording tape. It did so; the contents of the tape were immediately relayed into space; and Flandry listened with sharp interest to a playback.

It was a normal enough order, relating to certain preparations. Mind-hunter Svantozik of the Janneer Ya was departing for home as per command. He would not risk being spotted and traced back to Ardazir by some Terran, so would employ only a small ultra-fast flitter. (Flandry admired his nerve. Most humans would have taken at least a Meteor class boat.) The hour and date of his departure were given, in Urdahu terms.

"Rally 'round," said Flandry. The *Hooligan* glided into action.

He did not come near Vixen. That was the risky business of the liaison craft. He could predict the exact manner of Svantozik's take-off; there was only one logical way. The flitter would be in the middle of the squadron, which would roar spaceward on a foray. At the right time, Svantozik would give his own little boat a powerful jolt of primary drive; then, orbiting with cold engines away from the others, let distance accumulate. When he felt sure no Terran had spied him, he would go cautiously on gravs until well clear—then switch over into secondary and exceed the velocity of light. So small a craft, so far away from Walton's bases, would not be detected, especially with enemy attention diverted by the raiding squadron.

Unless, to be sure, the enemy had planted himself out in that region, with foreknowledge of Svantozik's goal and sensitive pulse-detectors running wide open.

When the alarm buzzed and the needles began to waver, Flandry allowed himself a yell. "That's our boy!" His finger stabbed a button. The *Hooligan* went into secondary with a wail of abused converters. When the viewscreens had steadied, Cerulia was visibly dimming to stern. Ahead, outlined in diamond constellations, the nebula roiled ragged black. Flandry stared at his instruments. "He's not as big as we are," he said, "but traveling like goosed lightning. Think we can overhaul short of Ardazir?"

"Yes, sir," said Chives. "In this immediate volume of space, which is dustier than average, and at these pseudo-speeds, friction becomes significant. We are more aerodynamic than he. I estimate twenty hours. Now, if I may be excused, I shall prepare supper."

"Uh-uh," said Flandry emphatically. "Even if he isn't aware of us yet, he may try evasive tactics on general principles. An autopilot has a randomizing predictor for such cases, but no poetry."

"Sir?" Chives raised the eyebrows he didn't have.

"No feel . . . intuition . . . whatever you want to call it. Svantozik is an artist of Intelligence. He may also be an artist at the pilot panel. So are you, little chum. You and I will stand watch and watch here. I've assigned a hairy great CPO to cook."

"Sir!" bleated Chives.

Flandry winced. "I know. Navy cuisine. The sacrifices we unsung heroes make for Terra's cause—!"

He wandered aft to get acquainted with his crew. Walton had personally chosen a dozen for this mission: eight humans; a Scothanian, nearly human-looking but for the horns in his yellow hair; a pair of big four-armed gray-furred shaggy-muzzled Gorzuni; a purple-and-blue giant from Donarr, vaguely like a gorilla torso centauroid on a rhinoceros body. All had Terran citizenship, all were career personnel, all had fought with every weapon from ax to operations analyzer. They were as good a crew as could be found anywhere in the known galaxy. And far down underneath, it saddened Flandry that not one of the humans, except himself, came from Terra.

The hours passed. He ate, napped, stood piloting tricks. Eventually he was close upon the Ardazirho boat, and ordered combat armor all around. He himself went into the turret with Chives.

His quarry was a squat, ugly shape, dark against the distant star-clouds. The viewscreen showed a slim blast cannon and a torpedo launcher heavier than most boats that size would carry. The missiles it sent had power enough to penetrate the *Hooligan's* potential screens, make contact, and vaporize the target in a single nuclear burst.

Flandry touched a firing stud. A tracer shell flashed out, drawing a line of fire through Svantozik's boat. Or, rather, through the space where shell and boat coexisted with differing frequencies. The conventional signal to halt was not obeyed.

"Close in," said Flandry. "Can you phase us?"

"Yes, sir." Chives danced lean triple-jointed fingers over the board. The *Hooligan* plunged like a stooping osprey. She interpenetrated the enemy craft, so that Flandry looked for a moment straight through its turret. He recognized Svantozik at the controls, in person, and laughed his delight. The Ardazirho slammed on pseudo-deceleration. A less skillful pilot would have shot past him and been a million kilometers away before realizing what had happened. Flandry and Chives, acting as one, matched the maneuver. For a few minutes they followed every twist and dodge. Then, grimly, Svantozik continued in a straight line. The *Hooligan* edged sideways until she steered a parallel course, twenty meters off.

Chives started the phase adjuster. There was an instant's sickness while the secondary drive skipped through a thousand separate frequency patterns. Then its in-an-out-of-space-time matched the enemy's. A mass detector informed the robot, within microseconds, and the adjuster stopped. A tractor beam clamped fast to the other hull's sudden solidity. Svantozik tried a different phasing, but the *Hooligan* equaled him without skipping a beat.

"Shall we lay alongside, sir?" asked Chives.

"Better not," said Flandry. "They might choose to blow themselves up, and us with them. Boarding tube."

It coiled from the combat airlock to the other hull, fastened leech-like with magnetronic suckers, and clung. The Ardazirho energy cannon could not be brought to bear at this angle. A missile flashed from their launcher. It was disintegrated by a blast from the *Hooligan's* gun. The Donarrian, vast in his armor, guided a "worm" through the boarding tube to the opposite hull. The machine's energy snout began to gnaw through metal.

Flandry sensed, rather than saw, the faint ripple which marked a changeover into primary drive. He slammed down his own switch. Both craft reverted simultaneously to intrinsic sub-light velocity. The difference of fifty kilometers per second nearly ripped them across. But the tractor beam held, and so did the compensator fields. They tumbled onward, side by side.

"He's hooked!" shouted Flandry.

Still the prey might try a stunt. He must remain with Chives, parrying everything, while his crew had the pleasure of boarding. Flandry's muscles ached with the wish for personal combat. Over the intercom now, radio voices snapped: "The worm's pierced through, sir. Our party entering the breach. Four hostiles in battle armor opposing with mobile weapons—"

Hell broke loose. Energy beams flamed against indurated steel. Explosive bullets burst, sent men staggering, went in screaming fragments through bulkheads. The Terran crew plowed unmercifully into the barrage, before it could break down their armor. They closed hand to hand with the Ardazirho. It was not too uneven a match in numbers; six to four, for half Flandry's crew must man guns against possible missiles. The Ardazirho were physically a bit stronger than humans. That counted little, when fists beat on plate. But the huge Gorzuni, the barbarically shrill Scothanian with his wrecking bar of collapsed alloy, the Donarrian happily ramping and roaring and dealing buffets which stunned through all insulation—they ended the fight. The enemy navigator, preconditioned, died. The rest were extracted from their armor and tossed in the *Hooligan's* hold.

Flandry had not been sure Svantozik, too, was not channeled so capture would be lethal. But he had doubted it. The Urdahu were unlikely to be that prodigal of their very best officers, who if taken prisoner might still be exchanged or contrive to escape. Probably Svantozik had simply been given a bloc against remembering his home sun's co-ordinates, when a pilot book wasn't open before his face.

The Terran sighed. "Clear the saloon, Chives," he said wearily. "Have Svantozik brought to me, post a guard outside, and bring us some refreshments." As he passed one of the boarding gang, the man threw him a grin and an exuberant salute. "Damn heroes," he muttered.

He felt a little happier when Svantozik entered. The Ardazirho walked proudly, red head erect, kilt somehow made neat again. But there was an inward chill in the wolf eyes. When he saw who sat at the table, he grew rigid. The fur stood up over his whole lean body and a growl trembled in his throat.

"Just me," said the human. "Not back from the Sky Cave, either, Flop down." He waved at the bench opposite his own chair.

Slowly, muscle by muscle, Svantozik lowered himself. He said at last, "A proverb goes: 'The hornbuck may run swifter than you think.' I touch the nose to you, Captain Flandry."

"I'm pleased to see my men didn't hurt you. They had particular orders to get you alive. That was the whole idea."

"Did I do you so much harm in the Den?" asked Svantozik bitterly.

"On the contrary. You were a more considerate host than I would have been. Maybe I can repay that." Flandry took out a cigarette. "Forgive me. I have turned the ventilation up. But my brain runs on nicotine."

"I suppose—" Svantozik's gaze went to the viewscreen and galactic night— "you know which of those stars is ours."

"Yes."

"It will be defended to the last ship. It will take more strength than you can spare from your borders to break us."

"So you are aware of the Syrax situation." Flandry trickled smoke through his nose. "Tell me, is my impression correct that you rank high in Ardazir's space service and in the Urdahu *orbekh* itself?"

"Higher in the former than the latter," said Svantozik dully. "The Packmasters and the old females will listen to me, but I have no authority with them."

"Still—Look out there again. To the Sky Cave. What do you see?"

They had come so far now that they glimpsed the thinner part of the nebula, which the interior luminosity could penetrate, from the side. The black cumulus shape towered ominously among the constellations; a dim red glow along one edge touched masses and filaments, as if a dying fire smoldered in some grotto full of spiderwebs. Not many degrees away from it, Ardazir's sun flashed sword blue.

"The Sky Cave itself, of course," said Svantozik wonderingly. "The Great Dark. The Gate of the Dead, as those who believe in religion call it. . . ." His tone, meant to be sardonic, wavered.

"No light, then? It is black to you?" Flandry nodded slowly. "I expected that. Your race is red-blind. You see further into the violet than I do; but in your eyes, I am gray and you yourself are black. Those atrociously combined red squares in your kilt all look equally dark to you." The Urdahu word he used for "red" actually designated the yellow-orange band; but Svantozik understood.

"Our astronomers have long known there is invisible radiation from the Sky Cave, radio and shorter wave lengths," he said. "What of it?"

"Only this," said Flandry, "that you are getting your orders from that nebula."

Svantozik did not move a muscle. But Flandry saw how the fur bristled again, involuntarily, and the ears lay flat.

The man rolled his cigarette between his fingers, staring at it. "You think the Dispersal of Ymir lies behind your own sudden expansion," he said. "They supposedly provided you with weapons, robot machinery, knowledge, whatever you needed, and launched you on your career of conquest. Their aim was to rid the galaxy of Terra's Empire, making you dominant instead among the oxygen breathers. You were given to understand that humans and Ymirites simply did not get along. The technical experts on Ardazir itself, who helped you get started, were they Ymirite?"

"A few," said Svantozik. "Chiefly, of course, they were oxygen breathers. That was far more convenient."

"You thought those were mere Ymirite clients, did you not?" pursued Flandry. "Think, though. How do you know any Ymirites actually were on Ardazir? They would have to stay inside a force-bubble ship all the time. Was *anything* inside that ship, ever, except a remote-control panel? With maybe a dummy Ymirite? It would not be hard to fool you that way. There is nothing mysterious about vessels of that type, they are not hard to build, it is only that races like ours normally have no use for such elaborate additional apparatus—negagrav fields offer as much protection against material particles, and nothing protects against a nuclear shell which has made contact.

"Or, even if a few Ymirites did visit Ardazir . . . how do you know they were in charge? How can you be sure that their oxygen-breathing 'vassals' were not the real masters?"

Svantozik laid back his lip and rasped through fangs, "You flop bravely in the net, Captain. But a mere hypothesis—"

"Of course I am hypothesizing." Flandry stubbed out his cigarette. His eyes clashed so hard with Svantozik's, flint gray striking steel gray, that it was as if sparks flew. "You have a scientific culture, so you know the simpler hypothesis is to be preferred. Well, I can explain the facts much more simply than by some cumbersome business of Ymir deciding to meddle in the affairs of dwarf planets useless to itself. Because Ymir and Terra have never had any serious trouble. We have no interest in each other! They know no terrestroid race could ever become a serious menace to them. They can hardly detect a difference between Terran and Merseian, either in outward appearance or in mentality. Why should they care who wins?"

"I do not try to imagine why," said Svantozik stubbornly. "My brain is not based on ammonium compounds. The fact is, however—"

"That a few individual Ymirites, here and there, have

performed hostile acts," said Flandry. "I was the butt of one myself. Since it is not obvious why they would, except as agents of their government, we have assumed that that was the reason. Yet all the time another motive was staring us in the face. I knew it. It is the sort of thing I have caused myself, in this dirty profession of ours, time and again. I have simply lacked proof. I hope to get that proof soon.

"When you cannot bribe an individual—blackmail him!"

Svantozik jerked. He raised himself from elbows to hands, his nostrils quivered, and he said roughly: "How? Can you learn any sordid secrets in the private life of a hydrogen breather? I shall not believe you even know what that race would consider a crime."

"I do not," said Flandry. "Nor does it matter. There is one being who could find out. He can read any mind at close range, without preliminary study, whether the subject is naturally telepathic or not. I think he must be sensitive to some underlying basic life energy our science does not yet suspect. We invented a mind-screen on Terra, purely for his benefit. He was in the Solar System, on both Terra and Jupiter, for weeks. He could have probed the inmost thoughts of the Ymirite guide. If Horx himself was not vulnerable, someone close to Horx may have been. Aycharaych, the telepath, is an oxygen breather. It gives me the cold shudders to imagine what it must feel like, receiving Ymirite thoughts in a protoplasmic brain. But he did it. How many other places has he been, for how many years? How strong a grip does he have on the masters of Urdahu?"

Svantozik lay wholly still. The stars flamed at his back, in all their icy millions.

"I say," finished Flandry, "that your people have been mere tools of Merseia. This was engineered over a fifteen-year period. Or even longer, perhaps. I do not know how old Aycharaych is. You were unleashed against Terra at a precisely chosen moment—when you confronted us with the choice of losing the vital Syrax Cluster or being robbed and ruined in our own sphere. You, personally, as a sensible hunter, would co-operate with Ymir, which you understood would never directly threaten Ardazir, and which would presumably remain allied with your people after the war, thus protecting you forever. But dare you co-operate with Merseia? It must be plain to you that the Merseians are as much your rivals as Terra could ever be. Once Terra is broken, Merseia will make short work of your jerry-built empire. I say to you, Svantozik, that you have been the dupe of your overlords, and that they have been the helpless, traitorous tools of Aycharaych. I think they steal off into space to get their orders from a Merseian gang—which, I think, I shall go and hunt!"

## CHAPTER XVII

As THE TWO flitters approached the nebula, Flandry heard the imprisoned Aidazirho howl. Even Svantozik, who had been before and claimed hard agnosticism, raised his ruff and licked dry lips. To red-blind eyes, it must indeed be horrible, watching that enormous darkness grow until it had gulped all the stars and only instruments revealed anything of the absolute night outside. And ancient myths will not die; within every Urdahu subconscious, this was still the Gate of the Dead. Surely, that was one reason the Merseians had chosen it for the lair from which they controlled the destiny of Ardazir. Demoralizing awe would make the Packmasters still more their abject puppets.

And then, on a practical level, those who were summoned —to report progress and receive their next instructions— were blind. What they did not see, they could not let slip, to someone who might start wondering about discrepancies.

Flandry himself saw sinister grandeur; great banks and clouds of blackness, looming in utter silence on every side of him, gulfs and canyons and steeps, picked out by the central red glow. He knew, objectively, that the nebula was near-vacuum even in its densest portions; only size and distance created that picture of caverns beyond caverns. But his eyes told him that he sailed into Shadow Land, under walls and roofs huger than planetary systems, and his own tininess shook him.

The haze thickened as the boats plunged inward. So too did the light, until at last Flandry stared into the clotted face of the infra-sun. It was a broad blurred disc, deep crimson, streaked with spots and bands of sable, hazing at the edges into impossibly delicate coronal arabesques. Here, in the heart of the nebula, dust and gas were condensing, a new star was taking shape.

As yet it shone simply by gravitational energy, heating as it contracted. Most of its titanic mass was still ghostly tenuous. But already its core density must be approaching quantum collapse, a central temperature of megadegrees. In a short time (a few million years more, when man was bones and not even the wind remembered him) atomic fires would kindle and a new radiance light this sky.

Svantozik looked at the instruments of his own flitter. "We orient ourselves by these three cosmic radio sources," he said pointing. His voice fell flat in a stretched quietness. "When we are near the . . . headquarters . . . we emit our call signal and a regular ground-control beam brings us in."

"Good." Flandry met the alien eyes, half frightened and half wrathful, with a steady compassionate look. "You know what you must do when you have landed."

"Yes." The lean grim head lifted. "I shall not betray anyone again. You have my oath, Captain. I would not have broken troth with the Packmasters either, save that I think you are right and they have sold Urdahu."

Flandry nodded and clapped the Ardazirho's shoulder. It trembled faintly beneath his hand. He felt Svantozik was sincere; though he left two armed humans aboard the prize, just to make certain the sincerity was permanent. Of course, Svantozik might sacrifice his own life to bay a warning, or he might have lied about there being only one installation in the whole nebula, but you had to take some risks.

Flandry crossed back to his own vessel. The boarding

tube was retracted. The two boats ran parallel for a time.

*Great unborn planets.* It had been a slim clue, and Flandry would not have been surprised had it proved a false lead. But . . . it has been know for many centuries that when a rotating mass has condensed sufficiently, planets will begin to take shape around it.

By the dull radiance of the swollen sun, Flandry saw his goal. It was, as yet, little more than a dusty, gassy belt of stones, strung out along an eccentric orbit in knots of local concentration, like beads. Gradually, the forces of gravitation, magnetism, and spin were bringing it together; ice and primeval hydrocarbons, condensed in the bitter cold on solid particles, made them unite on colliding, rather than shatter or bounce. Very little of the embryo world was visible; only the largest nucleus, a rough asteroidal mass, dark, scarred, streaked here and there by ice, crazily spinning; the firefly dance of lesser meteors, from mountains to dust motes, which slowly rained upon it.

Flandry placed himself in the turret by Chives. "As near as I can tell," he said, "this is going to be a terrestroid planet."

"Shall we leave a note for its future inhabitants, sir?" asked the Shalmuan, dead-pan.

Flandry's bark of laughter came from sheer tension. He added slowly, "It does make you wonder, though, what might have happened before Terra was born—"

Chives held up a hand. The red light pouring in turned his green skin a hideous color. "I think that is the Merseian beam, sir."

Flandry glanced at the instruments. "Check. Let's scoot."

He didn't want the enemy radar to show two craft. He let Svantozik's dwindle from sight while he sent the *Hooligan* leaping around the cluster. "We'd better come in about ten kilometers from the base, to be safely below their horizon," he said. "Do you have them located, Chives?"

"I think so, sir. The irregularity of the central asteroid confuses identification, but—Let me read the course, sir, while you bring us in."

Flandry took the controls. This would come as close to

seat-of-the-pants piloting as was ever possible in space. Instruments and robots, faster and more precise than live flesh could ever hope to be, would still do most of the work; but in an unknown, shifting region like this, there must also be a brain, continuously making the basic decisions. *Shall we evade this rock swarm at the price of running that ice cloud?*

He activated the negagrav screens and swooped straight for his target. No local object would have enough speed to overcome that potential and strike the hull. But sheer impact on the yielding force field could knock a small vessel galley west, dangerously straining its metal.

Against looming nebular curtains, Flandry saw two pitted meteors come at him. They rolled and tumbled, like iron dice. He threw in a double vector, killing some forward velocity while he applied a "downward" acceleration. The *Hooligan* slid past. A jagged, turning cone, five kilometers long, lay ahead. Flandry whipped within meters of its surface. Something went by, so quickly his eyes registered nothing but an enigmatic fire-streak. Something else struck amidships. The impact rattled his teeth together. A brief storm of frozen gases, a comet, painted the viewscreens with a red-tinged blizzard.

Then the main asteroid swelled before him. Chives called out figures. The *Hooligan* slipped over the whirling rough surface. "Here!" cried Chives. Flandry slammed to a halt. "Sir," added the Shalmuan. Flandry eased down with great care. Silence fell. Blackness lowered beyond the hull. They had landed.

"Stand by," said Flandry. Chives' green face grew mutinous. "That's an order," he added, knowing how he hurt the other being, but without choice in the matter. "We may possibly need a fast getaway. Or a fast pursuit. Or, if everything goes wrong, someone to report back to Walton."

"Yes, sir." Chives could scarcely be heard. Flandry left him bowed over the control panel.

His crew, minus the two humans with Svantozik, were already in combat armor. A nuclear howitzer was mounted on the Donarrian's centauroid back, a man astride to fire it.

The pieces of a rocket launcher slanted across the two Gorzuni's double shoulders. The Scothanian cried a war chant and swung his pet wrecking bar so the air whistled. The remaining five men formed a squad in one quick metallic clash.

Flandry put on his own suit and led the way out.

He stood in starless night. Only the wan glow from detector dials, and the puddle of light thrown in vacuum by a flashbeam, showed him that his eyes still saw. But as they adjusted, he could make out the very dimmest of cloudy red above him, and blood-drop sparks where satellite meteors caught sunlight. The gravity underfoot was so low that even in armor he was near weightlessness. Yet his inertia was the same. It felt like walking beneath some infinite ocean.

He checked the portable neutrino tracer. In this roil of nebular matter, all instruments were troubled; the dust spoke in every spectrum, a million-year birth cry. But there was clearly a small nuclear-energy plant ahead. And that could only belong to one place.

"Join hands," said Flandry. "We don't want to wander from each other. Radio silence, of course. Let's go."

They bounded over the invisible surface. It was irregular, often made slick by frozen gas. Once there was a shudder in the ground, and a roar traveling through their boot soles. Some giant boulder had crashed.

Then the sun rose, vast and vague on the topplingly near horizon, and poured ember light across ice and iron. It climbed with visible speed. Flandry's gang released hands and fell into approach tactics; dodging from pit to crag, waiting, watching, making another long flat leap. In their black armor, they were merely a set of moving shadows among many.

The Merseian dome came into view. It was a blue hemisphere, purple in this light, nestled into a broad shallow crater. On the heights around there squatted negafield generators, to maintain a veil of force against the stony rain. It had been briefly turned off to permit Svantozik's landing; the squat black flitter sat under a scarp, two kilometers from the dome. A small fast warcraft—pure Merseian, the final proof —berthed next to the shelter, for the use of the twenty or so beings whom it would accommodate. The ship's bow gun was aimed at the Ardazirho boat. Routine precaution, and there were no other defenses. What had the Merseians to fear?

Flandry crouched on the rim and tuned his radio. Svantozik's beam dispersed enough for him to listen to the conversation: "—no, my lords, this visit is on my own initiative. I encountered a situation on Vixen so urgent that I felt it should be made known to you at once, rather than delaying to stop at Ardazir—" Just gabble, bluffing into blindness, to gain time for Flandry's attack.

The man checked his crew. One by one, they made the swab-O-sign. He led them forward. The force field did not touch ground; they slithered beneath it, down the crater wall, and wormed toward the dome. The rough, shadow-blotted rock gave ample cover.

Flandry's plan was simple. He would sneak up close to the place and put a low-powered shell through. Air would gush out, the Merseians would die, and he could investigate their papers at leisure. With an outnumbered band, and so much urgency, he could not afford to be chivalrous.

"—thus you see, my lords, it appeared to me the Terrans—"

"*All hands to space armor! We are being attacked!*"

The shout ripped at Flandry's earphones. It had been in the Merseian Prime language, but not a Merseian voice. Somehow, incredibly, his approach had been detected.

"*The Ardazirho is on their side! Destroy him!*"

Flandry hit the ground. An instant later, it rocked. Through all the armor, he felt a sickening belly blow. It seemed as if he saw the brief thermonuclear blaze through closed lids and a sheltering arm.

Without air for concussion, the shot only wiped out Svantozik's boat. Volatilized iron whirled up, condensed, and sleeted down again. The asteroid shuddered to quiescence. Flandry leaped up. There was a strange dry weeping in his throat. He knew, with a small guiltiness, that he mourned more for Svantozik of the Janneer Ya than he did for the two humans who had died.

"—attacking party is about sixteen degrees north of the sunrise point, 300 meters from the dome—"

The gun turret of the Merseian warship swiveled about.

The Donarrian was already a-gallop. The armored man on his back clung tight, readying his weapon. As the enemy gun found its aim, the nuclear howitzer spoke.

That was a lesser blast. But the sun was drowned in its noiseless blue-white hell-dazzle. Half the spaceship went up in a fiery cloud, a ball which changed from white to violet to rosy red, swelled away and was lost in the nebular sky. The stern tottered, a shaken stump down which molten steel crawled. Then, slowly, it fell. It struck the crater floor and rolled earthquaking to the cliffs, where it vibrated and was still.

Flandry opened his eyes again to cold wan light. "Get at them!" he bawled.

The Donarrian loped back. The Gorzuni were crouched, their rocket launcher assembled in seconds, its chemical missile aimed at the dome. "Shoot!" cried Flandry. It echoed in his helmet. The cosmic radio noise buzzed and mumbled beneath his command.

Flame and smoke exploded at the point of impact. A hole gaped in the dome, and air rushed out. Its moisture froze; a thin fog overlay the crater. Then it began to settle, but with slowness in this gravitational field, so that mists whirled around Flandry's crew as they plunged to battle.

The Merseians came swarming forth. There were almost a score, Flandry saw, who had had time to throw on armor after being warned. They crouched big and black in metal, articulated tail-plates lashing their boots with rage. Behind faceless helmets, the heavy mouths might have been drawn into snarls. Their hoarse calls boomed over the man's earphones.

He raced forward. The blast from their sidearms sheeted over him. He felt heat glow through insulation, his nerves shrank from it. Then he was past the concerted barrage.

A dinosaurian shape met him. The Merseian held a blaster, focused to needle beam. Its flame gnawed at Flandry's cuirass. The man's own energy gun spat—straight at the other weapon. The Merseian roared and tried to shelter his gun with an armored hand. Flandry held his beam steady. The battle gauntlet began to glow. The Merseian dropped his blaster with a shriek of anguish. He made a low-gravity leap toward his opponent, whipped around, and slapped with his tail.

The blow smashed at Flandry. He went tumbling across the ground, fetched against the dome with a force that stunned him, and sagged there. The Merseian closed in. His mighty hands snatched after the Terran's weapon. Flandry made a judo break, yanking his wrist out between the Merseian's fingers and thumb. He kept his gun arm in motion, till he poked the barrel into the enemy's eye slit. He pulled trigger. The Merseian staggered back. Flandry followed, close in, evading all frantic attempts to break free of him. A second, two seconds, three, four, then his beam had pierced the thick superglass. The Merseian fell, gruesomely slow.

Flandry's breath was harsh in his throat. He glared through the drifting red streamers of fog, seeking to understand what went on. His men were outnumbered still, but that was being whittled down. The Donarrian hurled Merseians to earth, tossed them against rocks, kicked and stamped with enough force to kill them through their armor by sheer concussion. The Gorzuni stood side by side, a blaster aflame in each of their hands; no metal could long withstand that concentration of fire. The Scothanian bounced, inhumanly swift, his wrecking bar leaping in and out like a battle ax—strike, pry, hammer at vulnerable joints and connections, till something gave way and air bled out. And the humans were live machines bleakly wielding blaster and slug gun, throwing grenades and knocking Merseian weapons aside with karate blows. Two of them were down, dead; one slumped against the dome, and Flandry heard his pain over the radio. But there were more enemy casualties strewn over the crater.

The Terrans were winning. In spite of all, they were winning.

But—

Flandry's eyes swept the scene. Someone, somehow, had suddenly realized that a band of skilled space fighters was stealing under excellent cover toward the dome. There was no way Flandry knew of to be certain of that, without instruments he had not seen planted around. Except—

Yes. He saw the tall gaunt figure mounting a cliff. Briefly it was etched against the bloody sun, then it slipped from view.

Aycharaych had been here after all.

No men could be spared from combat, even if they could break away. Flandry bounded off himself.

He topped the ringwall in three leaps. A black jumble of rocks fell away before him. He could not see any flitting shape, but in this weird shadowy land eyes were almost useless at a distance. He knew, though, which way Aycharaych was headed. There was only one escape from the nebula now, and the Chereionite had gotten what information he required from human minds.

Flandry began to travel. Leap—not high, or you will take forever to come down again— long, low bounds, with the dark metallic world streaming away beneath you and the fire-coal sun slipping toward night again; silence, death, and aloneness. If you die here, your body will be crushed beneath falling continents, your atoms will be locked for eternity in the core of a planet.

A ray flared against his helmet. He dropped to the ground, before he had even thought. He lay in a small crater, blanketed with shadow, and stared into the featureless black wall of a giant meteor facing away from the sun. Somewhere on its slope—

Aycharaych's Anglic words came gentle, "You can move faster than I. You could reach your vessel before me and warn your subordinate I can only get in by a ruse, of course. He will hear me speak on the radio in a disguised voice of things known only to him and yourself, and will not see me until I have been admitted. And that will be too late for him. But first I must complete your life, Captain Flandry."

The man crouched deeper into murk. He felt the near-absolute cold of the rock creep through armor and touch his skin. "You've tried often enough before," he said.

Aycharaych's chuckle was purest music. "Yes. I really thought I had said farewell to you, that night at the Crystal Moon. It seemed probable you would be sent to Jupiter—I have studied Admiral Fenross with care—and Horx had been instructed to kill the next Terran agent. My appearance at the feast was largely sentimental. You have been an ornament of my reality, and I could not deny myself a final conversation."

"My friend," grated Flandry, "you're about as sentimental as a block of solid helium. You wanted us to know about your presence. You foresaw it would alarm us enough to focus our attention on Syrax, where you hinted you would go next—what part of our attention that superb red-herring operation had not fastened on Ymir. You had our Intelligence men swarming around Jupiter and out in the Cluster, going frantic in search of your handiwork, leaving you free to manipulate Ardazir."

"My egotism will miss you," said Aycharaych coolly. "You alone, in this degraded age, can fully appreciate my efforts, or censure them intelligently when I fail. This time, the unanticipated thing was that you would survive on Jupiter. Your subsequent assignment to Vixen has, naturally, proven catastrophic for us. I hope now to remedy that disaster, but—" The philosopher awoke. Flandry could all but see Aycharaych's ruddy eyes filmed over with a vision of some infinitude humans had never grasped. "It is not certain. The totality of existence will always elude us; and in that mystery lies the very meaning. How I pity immortal God!"

Flandry jumped out of the crater.

Aycharaych's weapon spat. Flame splashed off the man's armor. Reflex—a mistake, for now Flandry knew where Aycharaych was. The Chereionite could not get away—comforting to realize, than an enemy who saw twenty years ahead, and had controlled whole races like a hidden fate, could also make mistakes.

Flandry sprang up onto the meteor. He crashed against Aycharaych.

The blaster fired point-blank. Flandry's hand chopped down. Aycharaych's wrist did not snap across, the armor protected it. But the gun went spinning down into darkness. Flandry snatched for his own weapon. Aycharaych read the intention and closed in, wrestling. They staggered about on the meteor in each other's arms. The sinking sun poured its baleful light across them and Aycharaych could see better by it than Flandry. In minutes, when night fell, the man would be altogether blind and the Chereionite could take victory.

Aycharaych thrust a leg behind the man's and pushed. Flandry toppled. His opponent retreated. But Flandry fell slowly enough that he managed to seize the other's waist. They rolled down the slope together. Aycharaych's breath whistled in the radio, a hawk sound. Even in the clumsy spacesuit, he seemed like water, nearly impossible to keep a grip on.

They struck bottom. Flandry got his legs around the Chereionite's. He wriggled himself onto the back and groped after flailing limbs. A forearm around the alien helmet— he couldn't strangle, but he could immobilize and—His hands clamped on a wrist. He jerked hard.

A trill went through his radio. The struggle ceased. He lay atop his prisoner, gasping for air. The sun sank, and blackness closed about them.

"I fear you broke my elbow joint there," said Aycharaych. "I must concede."

"I'm sorry," said Flandry, and he was nothing but honest. "I didn't mean to."

"In the end," sighed Aycharaych, and Flandry had never heard so deep a soul-weariness, "I am beaten not by a superior brain or a higher justice, but by the brute fact that you are from a larger planet than I and thus have stronger muscles. It will not be easy to fit this into a harmonious reality."

Flandry unholstered his blaster and began to weld their

sleeves together. Broken arm or not, he was taking no chances. Bad enough to have that great watching mind next to his for the time needed to reach the flitter.

Aycharaych's tone grew light again, almost amused, "I would like to refresh myself with your pleasure. So, since you will read the fact anyway in our papers, I shall tell you now that the overlords of Urdahu will arrive here for conference in five Terran days."

Flandry grew rigid. Glory blazed within him. A single shell burst, and Ardazir was headless!

Gradually the stiffness and the splendor departed. He finished securing his captive. They helped each other up. "Come along," said the human. "I've work to do."

## CHAPTER XVIII

CERULIA did not lie anywhere near the route between Syrax and Sol. But Flandry went home that way. He didn't quite know why. Certainly it was not with any large willingness.

He landed at Vixen's main spaceport. "I imagine I'll be back in a few hours, Chives," he said. "Keep the pizza flying." He went lithely down the gangway, passed quarantine in a whirl of gold and scarlet, and caught an airtaxi to Garth.

The town lay peaceful in its midsummer. Now, at apastron, with Vixen's atmosphere to filter its radiation, the sun might almost have been Sol; smaller, brighter, but gentle in a blue sky where tall white clouds walked. Fields reached green to the Shaw; a river gleamed; the snowpeaks of the Ridge hovered dreamlike at world's edge.

Flandry looked up the address he wanted in a public telebooth. He didn't call ahead, but walked through bustling streets to the little house. Its peaked roof was gold above vine-covered walls.

Kit met him at the door. She stood unmoving a long time. Finally she breathed, "I'd begun to fear you were dead."

"Came close, a time or two," said Flandry, awkwardly.

She took his arm. Her hand shook. "No," she said, "y-y-you can't be killed. You're too much alive. Oh, come in, darlin'!" She closed the door behind him.

He followed her to the living room and sat down. Sunlight streamed past roses in a trellis window, casting blue shadows over the warm small neatness of furnishings. The girl moved about, dialing the public pneumo for drinks, chattering with frantic gaiety. His eyes found it pleasant to follow her.

"You could have written," she said, smiling too much to show it wasn't a reproach. "When the Ardazirho pulled out o' Vixen, we went back to normal fast. The mailtubes were operatin' again in a few hours."

"I was busy," he said.

"An' you're through now?" She gave him a whiskey and sat down opposite him, resting her own glass on a bare sunbrowned knee.

"I suppose so." Flandry took out a cigarette. "Until the next trouble comes."

"I don't really understan' what happened," she said. " 'Tis all been one big confusion."

"Such developments usually are," he said, glad of a chance to speak impersonally. "Since the Imperium played down all danger in the public mind, it could hardly announce a glorious victory in full detail. But things were simple enough. Once we'd clobbered the Ardazirho chiefs at the nebula, everything fell apart for their planet. The Vixen force withdrew to help defend the mother world, because revolt was breaking out all over their little empire. Walton followed. He didn't seek a decisive battle, his fleet being less than the total of theirs, but he held them at bay while our psychological warfare teams took Ardazir apart. Another reason for avoiding open combat as much as possible was that we wanted that excellent navy of theirs. When they reconstituted themselves as a loose federation of coequal *orbekhs*, clans, tribes, and what have you, they were ready enough to accept Terran supremacy—the Pax would protect them against each other!"

"As easy as that." A scowl passed beneath Kit's fair hair.

"After all they did to us, they haven't paid a millo. Not that reparations would bring back our dead, but should they go scot free?"

"Oh, they ransomed themselves, all right." Flandry's tone grew somber. He looked through a shielding haze of smoke at roses which nodded in a mild summer wind. "They paid ten times over for all they did at Vixen; in blood and steel and agony, fighting as bravely as any people I've ever seen for a cause that was not theirs. We spent them like wastrels. Not one Ardazirho ship in a dozen came home. And yet the poor proud devils think it was a victory!"

"What? You mean—"

"Yes. We joined their navy to ours at Syrax. They were the spearhead of the offensive. It fell within the rules of the game, you see. Technically, Terra hadn't launched an all-out attack on the Merseian bases. Ardazir, a confederacy subordinate to us, had done so! But our fleet came right behind. The Merseians backed up. They negotiated. Syrax is ours, now." Flandry shrugged. "Merseia can afford it. Terra won't use the Cluster as an invasion base. It'll only be a bastion. We aren't brave enough to do the sensible thing; we'll keep the peace, and to hell with our grandchildren." He smoked in short ferocious drags. "Prisoner exchange was a condition. All prisoners, and the Merseians meant all. In plain language, if they couldn't have Aycharaych back, they wouldn't withdraw. They got him."

She looked a wide-eyed question.

"Never mind," said Flandry scornfully. "That's a mere detail. I don't suppose my work went quite for nothing. I helped end the Ardazir war and the Syrax deadlock. I personally, all by myself, furnished Aycharaych as a bargaining counter. I shouldn't demand more, should I?" He dropped his face into one hand. "Oh, God, Kit, how tired I am!"

She rose, went over to sit on the arm of his chair, and laid a hand upon his head. "Can you stay here an' rest?" she asked softly.

He looked up. A bare instant he paused, uncertain himself. The rue twisted his lips upward. "Sorry. I only stopped in to say good by."

"What?" she whispered, as if he had stabbed her. "But, Dominic—"

He shook his head. "No," he cut her off. "It won't do, lass. Anything less than everything would be too unfair to you. And I'm just not the forever-and-ever sort. That's the way of it."

He tossed off his drink and stood up. He would go now, even sooner  than he had planned, cursing himself that he had been so heedless of them both as to return here. He tilted up her chin and smiled down into the hazel eyes. "What you've done, Kit," he said, "your children and their children will be proud to remember. But mostly . . . we had fun, didn't we?"

His lips brushed hers and tasted tears. He went out the door and walked down the street again, never looking back.

A vague, mocking part of him remembered that he had not yet settled his bet with Ivar del Bruno. And why should he? When he reached Terra, he would have another try. It would be something to do.


THE END